Virginia Andrews is a worldwide bestselling author. Her much-loved novels include RAIN, LIGHTNING STRIKES, EYE OF THE STORM and THE END OF THE RAINBOW. Virginia Andrews' novels have sold more than eighty million copies and have been translated into twenty-two foreign languages.

## The Dollanger Family Series

Flowers in the Attic
Petals on the Wind
If There Be Thorns
Seeds of Yesterday
Garden of Shadows

## The Casteel Family Series

Heaven
Dark Angel
Fallen Hearts
Gates of Paradise
Web of Dreams

## The Cutler Family Series

Dawn
Secrets of the Morning
Twilight's Child
Midnight Whispers
Darkest Hour

## The Landry Family Series

Ruby
Pearl in the Mist
All That Glitters
Hidden Jewel
Tarnished Gold

## The Logan Family Series

Melody
Heart Song
Unfinished Symphony
Music in the Night
Olivia

## The Orphans Mini-series

Butterfly
Crystal
Brooke
Raven
Runaways (full-length novel)

## The Wildflowers Mini-series

Wildflowers
Into the Garden

## The Hudson Family Series

Rain
Lightning Strikes
Eye of the Storm
The End of the Rainbow

## The Shooting Stars Series

Shooting Stars
Falling Stars

## The De Beers Family Series

Willow
Wicked Forest
Twisted Roots
Into the Woods
Hidden Leaves

My Sweet Audrina (does not belong to a series)

# VIRGINIA ANDREWS®

# HIDDEN LEAVES

POCKET
BOOKS

LONDON • NEW YORK • SYDNEY • TORONTO

First published in the US by Pocket Books, 2003
a division of Simon and Schuster Inc.
First published in Great Britain by Simon & Schuster UK Ltd, 2004
This edition published by Pocket Books, 2005
An imprint of Simon & Schuster UK Ltd
A Viacom Company

1 3 5 7 9 10 8 6 4 2

Simon & Schuster UK Ltd
Africa House
64–78 Kingsway
London WC2B 6AH

www.simonsays.co.uk

Simon & Schuster Australia
Sydney

A CIP catalogue record for this book is available from the British Library

ISBN 0-7434-6796-5
EAN 9780743467964

Printed and bound in Great Britain by
Bookmarque Ltd, Croydon, Surrey

# Contents

*To be given to my daughter, Willow, in the event of my death*

*Dr. Claude De Beers*

*Dear Willow,*

*Let me begin by first begging for your forgiveness. What you are about to learn should have been something you have known all you life. Just about every other child does or certainly should know. It has been the heaviest burden of my life carrying this secret inside me. The truth of it is your stepmother did not know this, either. There were times I feared she would come to suspect it, but ironically, her devotion to herself, her interest in herself blinded her. Actually, I think of the saying, "There are none so blind as those who will not see." She wouldn't look for these revelations. She wouldn't see them if they were right in front of her. Perhaps she was better off. Sometimes it is better to be in some ignorance.*

*I can't deny I was tempted to leave you in some ignorance, but I knew in my heart that would be unjust, untrue, unfair. What I did not have the courage to do is reveal the enclosed while I was still alive. There are so many reasons for my cowardice, I suppose, but none of them justifies it.*

*Even so, I beg for your forgiveness. Believe me when I tell you I have suffered more than you will, and believe me when I tell you my most important reason was always to be sure you would be a happy person. I hope and pray you still will be.*

*I know I never said it enough and it can never be said too much, but I want you to begin with this knowledge:*

*I love you, Willow.*

*I love you.*

*Daddy*

# 1

# In Love with a Patient

If someone had told me that someday I would fall in love with one of my patients, I would have recommended that he or she become one of my patients.

Now I have to admit that this most improbable event has occurred at my own clinic. It got so I couldn't wait to get there every morning. It was as if I had found that the doorway to paradise was always right in front of me. I quickly discovered that when you're with someone you love, the most mundane things suddenly become wonderful.

I suppose I'll never forget the day your mother arrived, Willow. She and I often talked about it, first as part of her therapy, and then, as time passed and our relationship grew into something I'm sure neither of us had expected, we were actually able to laugh about it.

You know how people often discuss what they were doing when some major historical event occurred. My father used to talk about where he was when the Japanese attacked Pearl Harbor, for example, and I often think about what I was doing the day President Kennedy was shot. Events like those are so imprinted on your mind it is as if life went on pause for a while and then began again.

Shall I tell you that when I first looked at your mother and she looked at me, my heart paused and then went on again? Shall I tell you that during those moments it felt as if there was no one else in the world but us? Does all this sound too romantic, perhaps more like the words in a love song than the words of a psychiatrist?

As a psychiatrist, I am too analytical, I know. I have a sort of love-hate relationship with my work. I don't really like to dissect people's emotions like some pathologist in a lab, but it is what I have been trained to do. Forgive me for how often I do that while writing this to you, Willow.

The truth is I remember everything about that day your mother arrived. It was unseasonably warm. Ordinarily I don't pay very much attention to the weather. I spend so much of my time indoors at the clinic, I don't care whether it's raining or not, whether it's cloudy or sunny, but for some reason (I hesitate to call it Fate or anything similar—it wouldn't be very professional of me) I remember sitting at my desk and looking out the window and admiring the soft, lithe look of a cloud moving lazily over the tops of the trees in front of my clinic. I don't daydream very often. I simply didn't have time for it with my patient load at the clinic, but that day it struck me that this was the only cloud in the eastern sky and I thought it looked lonely. I could even see a sad face in its fluffy surface and told myself something my mother used to tell me when I was a little boy: Rain, she said, was merely the teardrops of sad clouds, and when it stopped raining, we knew the clouds were happy again, sunshine lighting up their smiles.

"All smiles have to have sunshine behind them, Claude," she told me, "otherwise, they are not smiles; they are masks."

Perhaps that was my first lesson in psychiatry.

I laughed at myself for remembering such things and having such a thought—a cloud, lonely—but it brought back that wonderfully pure feeling of innocence. And then, suddenly there was your mother and grandmother's limousine coming in the front entrance and approaching the clinic.

I had a number of patients from well-to-do families, so I didn't think all that much of the fact that someone was bringing me a new patient in a fancy, luxurious limousine. Even though I don't have any hard and fast studies on the matter, I suppose I should tell you that I do believe wealthy people are more embarrassed by their mentally ill relatives, especially, unfortunately, parents who are embarrassed by their own children. They can't wait to drop them off here and pretend they are somewhere else.

Later, I discovered that was exactly what your

grandmother had done. She told people in Palm Beach, for that's where your mother and grandmother lived, that her daughter Grace was off again to college, only now out of state. Palm Beach, according to what your mother told me later, was one of those places where people can tell each other lies and feel confident they will be accepted as truth, at least on the surface. In her words, "It's just courteous to believe in someone else's fantasies. The richer they are, the more they believe in Santa Claus."

How clever she could be, don't you agree?

I watched her and your grandmother emerge from the long black limousine. Your grandmother wore a very stylish pink and white hat and indeed looked as if she was going to some ritzy charity event. Her teardrop earrings caught the sunlight and twinkled like tiny stars she might have plucked out of the Florida night sky. Even from my office window I could see she was an attractive woman, tall and stately with a runway model's posture when she walked. If she felt any shame, she wasn't about to let the world know it.

Your mother was difficult to evaluate from any distance, but especially difficult that day because she kept her head down, her shoulders turned inward, and her arms very close to her body, her hands crossed. This was not an unusual demeanor for me to see in one of my patients. People don't exactly come here because they are full of self-confidence.

Your mother and grandmother disappeared from my view when they walked to the front entrance. The driver followed with your mother's suitcases, and I sat back and continued to read her medical history, sent to me by her doctor in Palm Beach, a friend of mine, Dr. Anderson. I won't bore you with the medical terminology, the analysis and whatever. Suffice it to say, your mother was coming to me after having attempted suicide, but there were factors that told me she might very well not have realized the significance of what she was doing. I'll explain that later, and I promise, I won't be too technical.

While your mother was admitted, a process that involved some physical examination, recording of medications, etc., your grandmother was brought to my office. I usually meet with someone from the immediate family as soon as possible and preferably before I meet with the patient. Getting to know the parents, brothers, sisters, aunts, whoever, of a patient helps me understand what possible social and environmental factors are impacting on that patient.

Forgive me for writing about my work so seriously. I am trying not to be the doctor now, but your father instead, and, I suppose you have realized by now, I am not writing as your stepfather. I am writing as your biological father. I am your father, Willow, in every sense of the word. Your mother wasn't raped by some attendant as you were told too often by your stepmother, and I didn't bring you home because I felt guilty that such a thing happened at my clinic.

I have already told you how I was in love with one of my patients, your mother. I must now tell you how such a thing happened to a man who prided himself all his professional life in being objective, properly aloof, the doctor first and foremost. Your mother taught me that was not necessarily the best way for me to be, the best way for me to help my patients. In fact, dear Willow, everything gradually became reversed here between your mother and me. Many times toward the end, I felt more like the patient and your mother spoke to me with more wisdom than I had imagined she possessed.

But let me stop talking about what happened and talk about how it came to happen.

Into my office walked Jackie Lee Montgomery, your grandmother. I should say burst in, for she had that sort of confident, domineering presence. She was looking at everything like someone who was thinking about buying the clinic. It brought a smile to my face, but a smile I've learned to hide well under what you used to call my "doctor mask." There was just a slight quivering at the corners of my mouth as I told myself, *Claude De Beers, you'd better dot your i's and cross all your t's when you speak to this woman.*

My receptionist, Edith Hamilton, brought her to my office and announced her at the door.

"This is Mrs. Montgomery, Dr. De Beers," she said and stepped back, closing the door softly behind her.

I rose quickly to greet your grandmother, and she held out her hand like a queen who expected it to be kissed.

"Jackie Lee Montgomery," she said, holding her head high, her eyes fixed on mine.

"Please have a seat," I said, pulling a chair a little farther from the desk the way a gentleman would pull out a chair for his lady at a dining table. It made no sense for me to do that, but your grandmother had that sort of an effect on me. Later, I laughed about it with Grace. She told me her mother had become Palm Beachified. That was her term for it, for all the changes in her personality the wealth and the social life had caused.

"It breaks my heart to be bringing my daughter here, despite the wonderful references and recommendations I have received concerning you and this mental clinic, and despite how beautiful your building and location are," your grandmother Jackie Lee began.

"I understand, Mrs. Montgomery," I said, taking my seat.

"I'm sure you're wondering why I didn't return to my first married name or even my maiden name. My daughter was very fond of my second husband, Winston Montgomery. He adopted her and gave her his name, and I thought for the sake of simplicity, to avoid confusion . . ."

"Of course."

"I thought I should tell you that right away," she said.

"I understand completely," I said. "You made a wise decision."

"I would never keep my third husband's name," she said, pursing her lips so hard, it brought little spots of white at the corners of her mouth. "Dr. Anderson told me he has given you everything, so you are familiar with all that horror, I expect."

"I am, somewhat, yes."

She opened her purse and took out a frilled silk

handkerchief and brought it to her eyes even though I didn't see any tears.

"I've done the best I can dealing with this. What can anyone expect when a woman learns her husband has seduced, really raped her daughter in their own home, right under her very eyes practically?"

"It is quite overwhelming," I agreed.

"And Grace," she said, shaking her head and sighing, "hiding her pregnancy from me all that time until it was far too late to do anything about it." She paused and focused sharply on me as she leaned a bit forward. "Can you explain that to me? I never had a sensible explanation from Dr. Anderson for her behavior."

"Well, of course without speaking with Grace and exploring her troubles, it's difficult, Mrs. Montgomery. I can give you some classic reasons, which might very well be her reasons."

"What? What reason could anyone have for such behavior?" she practically pounced.

"First, of course, there's guilt. Too often women assume full or most of the responsibility for such things. To alleviate their own guilt and responsibility, some men often make them feel that way."

"He would," she said, spitting the words disdainfully at the floor.

"And if you have an impressionable young woman who has been through some additional mental crisis, she is more vulnerable to such chicanery."

"Chicanery. Exactly," she said, nodding, her eyes brightening with the way I sympathized with her situation.

"So keeping all that in mind, it wouldn't be all that unexpected for her not to hide her pregnancy so much as to go into complete self-denial."

"What do you mean by complete self-denial?"

"Try to convince herself it wasn't true, ignore the symptoms, and succeed enough at that to justify not telling you for a long time, as hard as it is for you to understand, Mrs. Montgomery."

"Jackie Lee, please."

"Jackie Lee. It's possible your daughter in all sense of the word actually believed she wasn't pregnant."

"Madness, utter madness. She does belong here."

"I saw from a note in her records that afterward you encouraged this in a way by pretending the child was yours. Am I correct that you actually simulated a pregnancy to persuade people it was so?"

She looked surprised that I knew that, but it was something that stood out in Dr. Anderson's report.

"I did what I did for her," she snapped back at me. "I was protecting her. You don't know how cruel and biting people are there. It was difficult enough trying to find her a decent man with whom she could develop a relationship. Imagine what this sort of sordid news would have done. I might as well have shipped her off to Somalia or some such godforsaken place."

I just nodded. Some people take that for agreement, and for the moment I could see it was better she assumed I approved of all she had done. In my experience, if you don't let parents, especially parents, come to their own conclusions as to their responsibility for the child's illnesses and problems, they will resent you and refuse to accept. Acceptance is the beginning of recovery.

There I go again, being the doctor. Sorry.

After I read the references to Jackie Lee's behavior, I had spoken with Dr. Anderson, of course, and he went into some detail about this cover-up Jackie Lee had created. He told me she became so absorbed in her own efforts to fool the public that, he thought, she had fooled herself as well. At least for a little while. He believed it contributed significantly to Grace's current depression and introversion. The truth is that the way he described your grandmother's behavior made it sound as if *she* should have been brought here as the patient and not your mother.

Now he was worried about the child, the little boy named Linden, growing up believing his grandmother was his mother. Dr. Anderson hoped I would help return Grace to a balanced enough state of mind so she could return and recapture her own child for both their sakes. It added pressure to my efforts, of course, and a solid reason for my letting her go. Neither of us could be selfish enough to see Linden without his mother. (It brings tears to my eyes just to write this, to write the words, *let her go,* for as you will see, that was just what I had to do.)

"Yes," I replied after a moment. "I'm sure what you did, you did for good reason, Jackie Lee."

She liked that and obviously liked I had stopped calling her Mrs. Montgomery.

"Exactly." She paused, dabbed her eyes again, and looked at me, her face turning dark and serious. "You don't think that it had a lot to do with what she . . . what she attempted to do to herself, do you?"

"It's best to wait for me to begin my examinations before we come to any conclusions about anything. I would be doing you a disservice to shoot from the hip, Jackie Lee. Give me some time."

"I know Dr. Anderson believes that it did. I could see it in his face whenever he spoke to me about it," she said, smirking. Then she sighed so deeply, I thought she had cracked her heart. "She was such a happy child once. When her father was alive, before his terrible helicopter accident, he doted on her and she practically worshiped the ground he walked upon. I was always warning him that he was spoiling her, not so much with gifts as with love. You can give someone too much love, you know.

" 'Grace will never be able to love any man because she will always compare him to you and find fault with him,' I warned him, but he didn't listen and that's exactly what happened."

She leaned toward me.

"You know she's not had one satisfactory romance and she's in her twenties!"

"It's not so unusual, Jackie."

"Jackie Lee."

"I'm sorry. Jackie Lee. Not unusual at all, especially these days," I said softly.

"It is for Grace. Wait until you see her. She's a very attractive young woman when she wants to be. Right now she looks like something the cat dragged home, but when she's had her hair fixed, especially by my stylists, and she puts on one of her designer dresses and has her makeup done properly, she's a little movie star. I saw the way men looked at her at charity events and parties.

"But she was always pushing them off for one reason or another," she said sadly. She nodded and then she stared at me a moment. "You know what she believes, don't you? I imagine it's down there in that report Dr. Anderson sent you," she said, nodding at the folder on my lap as though it were a criminal record instead of a doctor's file.

I didn't reply. I didn't want to reveal anything in Dr. Anderson's report.

"You don't have to read it. I'll tell you. She believes she carries a Jonah curse, that everyone or anyone who loves her or whom she loves will have something terrible happen to him or her. She'll tell you all about it, I'm sure, about all of them, her victims," she said, throwing her head back and rolling her eyes dramatically.

"We'll try to get her to think differently about herself," I said.

She sucked in her breath and sat straighter.

"Yes. Well, what do you think? Can you cure her? Will she ever be a normal woman and marry and have a family and a home?" she demanded.

"I hope so, Jackie Lee. It's my intention to make that a reality, yes. She does have a son to care for and raise, of course."

"Care for and raise," she muttered. "Well, I can't just toss him out there to be at the mercy of those sharks, now can I? For now, I'll continue being his mother."

"That might do him some harm in time, Jackie Lee. Perhaps you should think of how you can gradually get him to understand the truth," I suggested softly.

"Yes, well, we'll see. I don't want to make promises to him that will never be fulfilled. I know how mentally ill people can be, how their recoveries can be false or only temporary, especially someone in her condition. I've read a number of magazine articles about it."

"There is a lot of misinformation about that, Jackie Lee. Perhaps the old adage, 'A little knowledge is a dangerous thing' applies to this more than anything. Just be patient and give it all some time," I told her.

"Time. Exactly. How often should I come here?" she asked, rather demanded, I thought.

"Not for a while," I said. "Let's see how it goes and I'll call you."

She looked satisfied with that answer.

"I thought Grace was going to put up a fight or an argument about coming here, but she didn't so much as utter a little reluctance."

"That's good," I said.

"Good? Who would want to come here? How can that be something good?"

"Perhaps she realizes she needs help. That's what good, Jackie Lee. You have to recognize you have a problem before you can solve it."

"Um," she said. "Maybe. You know what she did, don't you? You know about her jumping off the dock in the middle of the night and then telling us she was getting on a ship with her dead father. She would have just let herself drown if we hadn't realized what she had done!"

"When people are so troubled, they lose their hold on what's real and what isn't. We all live in a little bit of illusion," I said, "but the difference is we know when to come back to reality."

"She doesn't," she said sharply.

"She will," I replied, now holding my eyes on her.

"I hope so," she relented. "Should I go back to say goodbye to her?"

"Maybe not. Maybe it's best you just leave quietly. She's in good hands. As you know, I have a wonderful staff here, and we don't like to see the families make the patients feel abandoned in any way."

"I'm not doing that," she retorted sharply.

"No, of course not, but someone who is already suffering with misconceptions, self-deprecation, loss of identity . . ."

"Yes, well, I suppose you are right. You do know more than I do," she said, standing.

"I'll walk you out," I said.

"It's a very pretty place. I mean, where it's located, those willow trees, the river nearby, the grounds."

"Nature is a true healer," I said.

"If that were true, you'd think the ocean would have been that for her. We lived right on the beach."

"It held other connotations, other meanings for her, perhaps."

"Her father crashed in the ocean, but we never

talked about that," she said, nodding. "Oh, this is all so complicated. It makes me spin."

"Don't worry. We'll sort it out," I said. "Did you want to see the rest of the clinic, our facilities?"

"No," she said quickly. "I'm sorry. I don't mean to sound disinterested, but seeing all these disturbed people, especially the younger ones, depresses me. I don't know how you do this sort of work, Doctor. How do you do it?"

"You think about helping them, seeing them walk out of here to be productive people again, and that's how you do it," I said.

I walked out with her to the waiting limousine. The moment the driver saw her, he jumped and rushed around to open the door for her. She had that sort of aura about her continuously, commanding.

"This isn't easy for me," she said at the car, looking back at the clinic and taking a deep breath. "She's my only child. Aside from poor Linden, of course."

"I understand," I said.

"I keep thinking about how happy we all were when our lives were chaotic, when we were moving from naval base to naval base, following my husband in his career, never really having any roots. They used to salute each other, you know," she said. "With two fingers. She did it when she was only two, and he thought it was so funny and cute that he never forgot and always did it the same way."

I smiled.

She was really crying now, and I thought that under the shell she had created for herself in order, perhaps, to survive in the world she had found herself living in now, she still had a very warm, loving other self, desperately trying to be heard. When we're honest about our own emotions, we have the best chance for happiness, Willow. Always remember that.

I squeezed her hand gently.

She looked at me one more time and in a whisper said, "Take care of my baby."

Then she got into that luxurious, shiny black limousine with its tinted windows. I actually felt sorry for her. She looked shut up, locked away in there. The windows reflected me and the clinic. I no longer saw her, and moments later she was driven away.

I watched her go, and then I turned back to my clinic and walked with determined steps to attack whatever monster resided in your mother's troubled mind.

# 2

# A Little Footnote

After her admittance your mother was shown to her room and then given a little tour of our clinic before she was brought to my office. My head nurse, Nadine Gordon, took her around. We always tried to give the patients a sense of security, a sense of comfort before we began any formal therapy and treatment. It's not easy for a healthy person to leave home and find himself or herself in a strange new world, much less someone who was already quite fragile and unpredictable.

Nurse Gordon knocked on my door and then brought Grace into my office.

"This is Dr. Claude De Beers," she said. She always introduced me with such pomp and circumstance in her voice that made me feel, and I'm sure my new patient feel, as if I sat atop a mountain.

When I told her she always introduced me as though I was someone high and mighty, she replied, "That's what they should think of you, Doctor. The more confidence a patient has in her doctor, the better chance she has of becoming well," she advised. She was not above lecturing even me.

She was very hard on the younger psychiatrists who tried to be pals with their patients. Most of them were actually afraid of her. You can just imagine what she came to think of my relationship with your mother, but that's something I'll talk about later. I feel like a schoolboy who is so excited about getting out his story, he can't keep himself from jumping ahead. (A bit of self-analysis here, I'm afraid. The inherent danger of being a psychiatrist.) I hope, whenever you're reading this, that this little footnote brings a smile to your face, Willow.

"Hello, Grace," I said. "I've been looking forward to meeting you."

Your mother looked up at me with eyes that spoke volumes. Page one was full of skepticism. Why would I look forward to meeting her? Why would anyone? I could see the questions so clearly, I actually heard them as well.

"Dr. De Beers said hello," Nurse Gordon told her, as if she were my translator.

"That will be all," I said, dismissing her. "Thank you Ms. Gordon,"

She gave me her sharp professional gaze for a moment and then softened, permitted her lips to weaken into a small smile, and left the office, taking so long to close the door, she appeared reluctant to do so. I could see the way Grace watched her every move. That told me her being introverted did not keep her from being observant and aware of her surroundings.

"Won't you sit here," I said, nodding at the sofa. "It's more comfortable."

I didn't like sitting behind my desk, especially when I spoke to my patients. It made me feel I was behind some wall and very distant from them. You remember how big my desk was, too. Even a man my size looks wrapped in wood.

She sat and I sat across from her.

"Oh, would you like something to drink, Grace, soda, juice, water?" I asked her.

She shook her head. I remember immediately being captured by those eyes, the softest turquoise eyes I had ever seen, beautiful, vulnerable, desperately searching for someone to trust, another heart in which to place her hopes and dreams safely. At that moment she reminded me of a small bird, so helpless and yet so capable of love, so eager to soar, perhaps right under that lonely cloud I had seen earlier.

"We should first simply get to know each other," I told her. "I know a little about you, of course, but I am hoping you will tell me much more."

She waited, shifting her eyes nervously to avoid mine. Isn't it interesting how no one likes to be stared at normally, Willow? People who are suffering inside especially hate being observed. I looked at her file and tried at first to speak to her without looking at her directly, hoping that would put her at some ease. But I must also tell you that was difficult for me, for I wanted to look at her very much.

"My, you did travel a lot when you were younger, didn't you? All these places, all these new schools to attend, new friends to make. It must have been hard for you when you were so young. I know it would have been for me," I said. "I was fortunate in that we lived where my father's father lived and in fact, my great-grandfather as well. I'm still living there, in fact," I told her. "But you . . ." I shook my head.

And for the first time her eyes widened with a little interest and her eyebrows rose.

"Matter of fact," I continued, "I don't think I know anyone who has moved around as much as you have. You're the first Gypsy in my office," I added, and she smiled.

For me that first breakthrough with a patient is always the most delicious and satisfying.

"My daddy called us Gypsies."

"Did he? Tell me about him. He was a commander in the Naval Air Force, a helicopter pilot?"

"Yes."

"I can't imagine him liking being away from you and your mother so often."

"He hated that, but he had to follow orders. 'We all have to follow orders, Sailor Girl,' he would say."

"Sailor Girl?"

I knew why she used that term for herself. Dr. Anderson had it in his notes, but it was far better to have the patient retell it.

"That's what he called me," she said. Her smile was deeper, softer, full of memories.

I know I was staring at her like a schoolboy stares at his first love, Willow. She noticed and looked at me strangely, and I realized it. I think, and I know you will be amazed, I actually blushed, not something I do very often.

"You're not what I expected," she said.

"Oh? Why is that?"

"You're not old. I thought you would be older."

"Why?"

"You have your own clinic and everything and my doctor in Palm Beach looks older than you do and he made you sound like you were his mentor."

I laughed.

"Well, I've been lucky. This place practically fell into my lap."

"He told me you go around the country lecturing and that you were brilliant," she said.

"Let's reserve judgment on that," I told her. "First, let's see if I can help you. If I can do that, then we'll consider it," I said, and she nearly laughed. I saw it in her eyes. Sometimes, you just know quickly you're going to like someone and he or she is going to like you. It's as if the both of you have the correct combination to that lock that keeps our most private selves hidden from most people.

"Tell me about those early years in your life. How did you feel about all this moving around, changing schools, constantly making friends?"

"I didn't mind it. I was better off then."

"Why?" I asked her.

"I didn't have close friends. I didn't have anyone to mourn," she said.

"Mourn? Why do you say that?"

I thought she wasn't going to answer. She looked away and then she turned back to me, her eyes narrowing, just the way yours do, Willow, when you get intense about something.

"We had a dog once, a golden retriever called Kasey," she said. "She was hit by a car when she was only four and killed."

"How sad for you."

"Mommy cried and so did I and Daddy was very depressed. He loved that dog. And then Mommy said, 'I'll never have another dog. I'm not going through this again, this terrible loss,' and we never did," she said. "She had less to mourn."

"Did that make you unhappy? I mean, didn't you want another dog?"

"No."

"Why not? Was it because you wanted your mother to be happy?"

"Yes, but it was more than just that."

"Tell me," I said, leaning toward her. I felt like holding her hand in mine.

"We take a risk anytime we give anything or anyone our love," she said, and I thought, what a remarkable observation. She might be a very troubled person, but she was also a very sensitive and perceptive one. I knew it that first day I met her.

"That's true," I said. "But if it's someone or something worth the risk, then we should take it, don't you think?"

She looked away again, and when she looked back at me I saw that her face had grown darker. I could see the light in her eyes diminish as she turned inward on her own troubled thoughts. Sometimes it takes a while to open that curtain and see all that is twisted and troubling inside someone, Willow, and sometimes, as it was with your mother, it comes almost immediately.

"Nothing, no one is worth that risk," she said.

"Why do you say that so firmly, Grace? Haven't you loved other people since your father's death? You seemed to have been very fond of your stepfather, Winston Montgomery," I said, noting Anderson's comments in her file.

"And look what happened to him."

"He wasn't a young man when he died."

"He wasn't an old man, either," she retorted. I could see the fury in her eyes now, but it was a fury she was directing at herself then, Willow.

"No, he wasn't, but people get sick and sometimes it isn't anyone's fault. That's true, too, isn't it, Grace?"

She didn't answer, and when she didn't want to answer, she turned away so I couldn't see the thin, glassy shelf of tears cover her eyes.

It's so important to get a patient to believe he or she isn't so much unlike you or everyone else. You have to create that bond and that trust.

"I remember when my mother died," I began, and she turned back to me slowly. "I was finished with medical school and I kept thinking I should have noticed something. I should have been there for her. I blamed myself and for a long time, too."

She raised her eyebrows again.

"What happened to her?"

"She had a stroke, a massive cerebral stroke. Thankfully, she wasn't in a coma long."

"That was different," she said after a moment.

"Why?"

"You thought you should have seen physical things and gotten her some medicine. You didn't bring her bad luck."

"Why should someone have the power to bring someone else bad luck?" I asked her.

"It's not a power; it's a curse!"

"Why should someone have such a curse put on her?"

"Fate decides that before you're born," she told me.

I didn't smile. I nodded. "Well, that's something you will have to explain more to me."

"I don't want to," she said and pressed her lips together like a defiant child.

"I can wait until you do," I said.

She threw a furious look my way, and I could see she was getting angry at me, so I looked at her file and then looked at the clock.

"I bet you're tired with the trip here and all, aren't you?"

She nodded.

"We have lots of time to talk. Did you get a good tour of our clinic?"

She shrugged. "That nurse moved and spoke very fast."

"Yes, she can be that way," I said, smiling. "I'll call Nurse Gordon and ask her to show you back to your room," I said, and then I decided no, I'll show her back. "Why don't I escort you, myself," I said. She looked happier about that. "It isn't all that much longer until dinner. I'm sure you'd like a little rest first, take a shower, change your clothes, do whatever you want."

"I can't do exactly whatever I want," she replied. "Your nurse made that very clear with her list of rules."

"Well, whatever she told you is designed to keep you and the others here safe, but we don't want you to feel like you're shut away, Grace. This is simply a place where all the people who can help you come together and concentrate on you. Give it a chance," I urged.

She nodded and stood. Her eyes perused the office, and she saw the picture I had of your stepmother. I saw the curiosity in her face.

"Is that your wife?"

"Yes, Alberta," I said.

"She's very pretty," she said.

"Yes. Thank you."

"Do you have any children?"

"No. Not because I don't want any," I added quickly.

She looked at me sharply for a moment, and then I opened the door and we walked down the corridor.

Funny first meeting with the woman I would soon love more than any woman, wasn't it, Willow? We used to think so. It was hardly a romantic encounter. No music, no beautiful setting, no innocent laughter and carefree feelings. Instead, we were in my office with me being Mr. Psychiatrist.

You can't imagine how amusing your mother was when she imitated me, imitated my techniques, as she liked to call my little gestures and mannerisms. No one made me see myself clearer than your mother did, Willow. Through her eyes I finally understood who I was and for that, I would always be grateful to her. After she was gone, I often thought she had given me far more than I had given her.

I walked her past the arts and crafts room, which I noticed she looked at with some interest, and then we paused at the doorway of her room. She stood there looking in at it, hesitating. Our rooms were far from spartan. They all had pretty curtains, nice furniture, lots of brightness with the windows and the pleasant coffee-white walls, all of which had paintings on them, beautiful scenes of Nature, peaceful, meditative. The floors were carpeted, and each room had its own bathroom. Patients had to go to the entertainment center to watch television. We had game tables there, cards and checkers and chess boards, and a good library. We didn't want them spending too much time alone, you see.

But this was not home and I was sure quite a bit different from the bedroom your mother had at her home. She had brought along some of her personal things, which I learned included a number of presents her father had brought home to her from his various naval excursions. One of them was a teddy bear she already had on the bed.

I always prided myself in having great compassion for my patients, Willow, but seeing your mother standing there in the doorway of her clinic room, her eyes filling with the realization that this was her home for now and for perhaps a long, long time, practically brought tears to my eyes. I recognized immediately that I was feeling everything more deeply when it involved her. I didn't ignore it, but I did try not to pay any attention to it. Little did I know then how terribly I would fail at that. However, that was one personal failure I do not regret, even to this day, Willow.

She turned and looked at me.

"What sort of a person was here before me?" she asked.

"A young woman, not unlike yourself."

"What was wrong with her?"

"Serious mood swings. What we call bipolar."

"Is that what's wrong with me?"

"Let's wait and see, spend more time before we make any definitive diagnosis."

She smirked a bit, but that was a truthful answer on my part.

"Whatever happened to her?" she asked, nodding at the bed as if the previous patient were still there.

"She's home now with her family and she's doing well. Just like you will," I said.

She smiled, but it was the smile of someone humoring someone.

She didn't have to say the words. I could hear them: "Yeah, sure. Tell me another fairy tale."

Nothing stirred my determination more. Right then and there I swore to myself: *I will make her healthy and well enough to take care of herself again. She will go home to her child.*

# 3

# A Forgotten Social Event

It wasn't often that I remained at the clinic and had dinner with my staff or with some of our patients, but I very much wanted to that first night your mother arrived. Your stepmother Alberta was already quite annoyed with me because of how much time I was devoting to the clinic. She went so far as to accuse me of adultery, claiming I was more in love with it than I was with her. We were only married a short time before I was able to put the clinic together, and it was a very exciting opportunity for me at the time.

Even from the very beginning, I don't think your stepmother ever really respected the work I did, Willow. Oh, she liked the fact that she was married to a doctor, especially one who had something of a national reputation, but either she was frightened by my work or she was simply bored with it, for she hated my bringing home any stories about the clinic and especially anything at all to do with any and all of my patients.

Ironically, her father had no respect for psychiatric medicine. He thought it was all a way to excuse people from their responsibilities and called it voodoo medicine. However, he looked upon our marriage very favorably. Of course my sister, your aunt Agnes, attributed all that to my father-in-law's poor economic situation. Alberta came from an old Southern family who had become land rich and dollar poor, and they were gradually losing all of their property, selling it off to developers in order to survive.

As you know from our photographs and news clippings, Alberta was a beautiful young woman when we married. Whenever there was any sort of charity event that involved modeling clothing, she was asked to be part of it. She might even have gone on to do that professionally, but her mother and especially her paternal grandparents believed modeling to be a profession just a step away from prostitution. Quite a ridiculous and old-fashioned way of thinking, but nevertheless, a way of thinking that heavily influenced Alberta.

I won't tell you that I was ever deeply in love with your stepmother, but I will say that she fascinated me. She always maintained a true Southern elegance about her. In my way of thinking, she was one of those people who were truly born in the wrong century, who belonged at a far different historical period, like someone who had literally stepped out of *Gone With the*

*Wind* or some such novel. I used to think she laughed like Scarlett O'Hara. Her beauty easily made her the catch of the season at her debutante ball.

I can't recall exactly who said it, but someone told me, "A man like you should have a wife like that, Claude," and that stuck in my mind. We were truly a famous couple during those early years, invited to everything, our pictures always on the social pages. A doctor is like anyone else: dependent upon image, reputation, recommendations. Of course, he has to have ability and knowledge, but many, many do and yet do not find the level of success I have found, and some of that might be attributed to my high social profile, what some people call networking. It certainly helped me get the financing I needed and opened many a door quickly.

If I was to analyze myself, Willow, I would have to admit to being a little insecure and perhaps too dependent on and grateful for the public image. It's very easy to fall in love with your own public self. You're complimented and lauded so much, you begin to believe your own publicity. Thankfully, I believe I caught hold of myself before it was too late and stepped back and away from all the empty glitter, something for which, I'm afraid, your stepmother never forgave me. I became less and less her husband and more and more the doctor. Maybe that was the real reason why she came to hate my work and the clinic so much.

It wasn't long before your mother had come to my clinic that Alberta and I began to lead quite separate lives. She didn't want to be part of what I was, and I didn't want to be part of her social world. To me it seemed a great waste of valuable time, frivolous and full of self-important people.

I can't tell you how many times she said, "Why can't you be like the other doctors in this community, Claude, and have office hours and answering services that keep people away?"

You heard her say things like that, I'm sure. Sometimes, I wondered if she wasn't right. Had I become obsessed with my work to the detriment of everything else in my life? I suppose if I feel guilty about anything, Willow, it's not spending enough time with you. I depended too much on your Amou, your beloved nanny.

Getting back to that wonderful first day I met your mother, however, I must describe what happened at dinner. At the clinic we encouraged as much interaction among the patients as was not only possible, but beneficial. As you know from some of the things I've told you, I've had patients who were so outgoing we practically had to keep them in chains, and patients who were so introverted, so closed up, they practically had to be hand-fed. Your mother was never that bad, but it was easy to see she wanted to keep to herself.

She tried to sit alone at a table that first night, but Nurse Gordon would not permit it. To be fair to her, it was our policy to try to get the patients not to withdraw, and she was doing only what we considered good therapy. Occasionally, one or more of my associates had dinner with the patients, and I had on occasion as well, so it wasn't so unusual for me to do the same. Even so, Nurse Gordon looked very surprised when I appeared in the dining room. There were no other physicians there this particular evening. Dr. Ralston Price and I were the head physicians and he was off to speak at a convention.

We had nearly twenty patients in the clinic at the time, their ages ranging from fourteen to sixty-eight. One was a young woman about your mother's age. I'll call her Sandy because she had flaxen blond hair that she kept long and stringy and pulled on with such force sometimes, it made her forehead crimson. Sometimes she actually pulled out some strands and held them in her small, tight fist like threads of real gold. At night Nurse Gordon would practically have to pry her fingers open with a crowbar, and Sandy would scream and threaten to bite her. That was a confrontation to behold. Nadine Gordon was no one easily intimidated, however. She usually got her way.

Sandy was an obsessive-compulsive, and she could, if she targeted someone, talk incessantly at him or her, regardless of whether or not the recipient of her conversation actually paid her any attention. She was at your mother that first night and on about her favorite new topic: the dark figures she saw lurking about the clinic, looking, she believed, for an opportunity to crawl into people.

She sat beside your mother and began to polish her silverware clean. If someone didn't remind her to eat, she would sit there all night polishing her fork and her spoon.

"I saw them bring you here," she told Grace. "They knew you were coming. They were whispering about you in the corridor all day, you know. They're just waiting outside your room now. You don't look at them. You don't let them look into your eyes. That's very important. When you see them, you turn away," she warned. "You give them your back and don't ever, ever walk into a dark room. They have you where they want you if you do that. You can't see them in the dark. That makes sense, doesn't it?

"They followed me here, you know. They followed me. But don't blame me for them. They followed other people, too. They followed you, I bet. Didn't they?"

Your mother looked a bit terrified.

"Sandy," I said, sitting down across from her, "I want you to start eating. You want time to do other things tonight, and besides, we can't keep the kitchen staff waiting for you all night, can we?"

She looked at me, looked at Grace, and then she started to polish her fork.

"Sandy, start eating," I said a little more firmly.

All the while your mother was watching, fascinated, but still obviously frightened, too.

Nurse Gordon came up behind Sandy and threatened to take her fork and have her eat with her hands. She wouldn't eat if we did that anyway, of course. She would go out to wash them and spend an hour in the bathroom doing so.

"C'mon, Sandy," I coached. "See, Grace is eating. She wants to finish and do other things."

She looked at Grace and then she took a small fork

full of mashed potatoes, inspecting it closely before putting it into her mouth.

"I'm tired," she said almost immediately after one fork full.

"So eat and then go to sleep," Nurse Gordon told her. She oversaw the patients at the tables with an eagle eye and with catlike movements.

"If there's something in particular you like to eat, just let the nurse know," I told Grace. "We have an excellent chef."

I saw Nurse Gordon's eyebrows rise. It wasn't something I told every patient, of course. I had to evaluate each one and what he or she would want to know and of course was capable of knowing.

"Sometimes you make this place sound like a country club, Dr. De Beers," Nurse Gordon told me later.

"I just want them to feel comfortable here," Ms. Gordon," I replied.

"If they're too comfortable, they'll never want to leave," she retorted.

She could be a hard person, but she was so efficient and so competent, I couldn't think of letting her go.

Afterward, I walked your mother out and tried to get her to relax a while, watch some television perhaps, or read in the recreation room, but she complained about being too tired and just wanted to sleep. Of course, she was in a deep depression and people who are often choose sleep over anything or everything else. I suppose it's a form of escape. (I could write on and on about this and have to keep reminding myself this isn't an article for a psychology magazine.)

I escorted her to her room again. I do try to give each and every one of my patients as much personal attention as I can, but I recognized that I was trying to find every way possible to remain with Grace.

"Your room has one of the nicer views. It looks toward the Congaree River. I can walk to it from my home, but because of our height here, we can catch glimpses of it. I know you had the ocean to look at, but it's nice to have water nearby, even if it's only a river," I told her.

She looked at me with what I thought were smiling eyes. She could sense my struggle to keep talking, to find a way quickly to break through the dark curtain she had dropped between herself and the world.

"I don't look outside much anymore," she said.

"Well, we'll just have to help you do that, then," I told her.

She seemed to sink inside herself, retreat into those dark places that sadly had become her comfort zone. I wished her a good night just as Nurse Gordon came down to dispense her medication.

"Still here, Doctor?" she asked, a bit surprised.

"Just on my way out," I said and said good night to Grace. She didn't look at me. I exchanged a quick, doctor's-mask look with Nurse Gordon and then left.

About a year before your mother arrived at the clinic, I hired a former patient of mine to be my driver and to fulfill some of our household chores which involved mainly looking after the grounds. His name is Miles Porter, and I imagine he will still be with us when you read this. Alberta was against my hiring him because he was a former patient of mine, but I held fast to my decision and she accepted it, even though she never treated him with much respect and often complained about what she considered his strange silences and his work. She avoided him and Miles didn't miss any opportunity to avoid Alberta.

Because I had remained at the clinic for dinner, Miles ate with the staff.

He was used to my working in the car, reading or scribbling notes, but I couldn't help wondering if even Miles saw something different in me that night. Willow, can I tell you my heart was pounding? I didn't feel foolish as much as I felt guilty, like someone caught being where he knew he shouldn't be. *Why do I feel this way?* I continually asked myself as we drove home that night. I had met a new patient. I had helped her begin to orient herself to her new surroundings. I had a preliminary session with her. I had given her a little tender loving care. *I've done that before, haven't I?* My driver, Miles, sitting in front, was a prime example of that.

*All true,* I heard my inner self reply, *but why can't you get that young woman's eyes and soft lips out of your mind? This imagery doesn't have anything to do with your work or her needs. I'm surprised at you, Claude De Beers. You're behaving like a lovesick schoolboy. Get hold of yourself.*

There I was holding a full, all-out debate with myself in the car.

Your stepmother wasn't home when we arrived. I was grateful for that. I felt as if I had another woman's lipstick on my collar or something and all she would have had to do was look at my face and point her finger at me and ask, "What have you been doing, Claude? Why do you have that look on your face?"

It was ridiculous of me to think that, of course. If anyone was oblivious to my moods, my looks, it was Alberta. Most of the time she was so occupied with her own activities and thoughts, she wouldn't know if I was there or not. I didn't think about where she was this particular evening. She was often somewhere when I returned from the clinic, but when she arrived this particular evening, she marched right to my office where I was catching up on some paperwork and stood in the doorway glaring in at me.

"How do you feel about yourself now?" she asked.

I tell you, Willow, my heart skipped beats. If guilty feelings popped out on one's face, I would have been covered in red freckles.

"What?"

I wondered: Could someone have called her from the clinic and said something to her about my behavior toward Grace? That's how guilty and self-conscious I felt.

"I don't understand, Alberta," I continued. I think I was holding my breath, too.

"I just want to know how you feel about yourself? About not having the decency to at least call to say you weren't going to be there."

I shook my head.

"I'm sorry, Alberta, be where?"

"Be where?" She looked away for a moment, calming herself. She actually looked more beautiful when she was angry like this. Her face would take on a soft ruby tint, and her eyes would blaze with the fire of rage stoked inside her. "How about the executive committee for the Heart Association gala ball? You and I are sponsors as well. Your name was prominent on the program, Claude."

"Oh. Oh, yes," I said, glancing at the formal invitation stuck between the pages of a medical reference book on my desk. She had made a point of giving the invitation to me so I wouldn't forget it, and I had put it in my calendar. In fact, I had even remembered it that morning on my way to the clinic and had made a mental note about what time I wanted to leave to get home to dress. As I told you, I avoided as many of these dinners as I could, but I recognized this one was special, especially for Alberta.

"Oh, yes? Do you have any idea what it was like for me to be seated next to an empty chair? Bart Kaplow thought it was funny and suggested we talk to the chair as if you were in it. I told him it wouldn't be anything new for me. I often talk to the walls at home."

"I'm sorry, Alberta. I had a new patient arrive late in the day and—"

"I see. And what I want, what I need, is not as important. I know. You don't have to confirm it. Thank you, Claude, for clearly illustrating where I stand on your totem pole of priorities."

She reached in for my door handle and pulled it shut, the sound like a clap of thunder. I sat there staring at the door wondering what indeed had happened to me that I would have completely forgotten this social event. It actually frightened me a little, and I made a secret promise to myself that when I returned to the clinic in the morning, I would be more my professional self than I had ever been. For now, I wouldn't attempt any more apologies, I thought. Alberta was too angry at me.

As you will remember, your stepmother and I had separate bedrooms. There was an adjoining door, but our relationship with each other eventually cooled to the point where that door was rarely, if ever, unlocked.

The idea of separate bedrooms was something Alberta thought romantic in the early days of our marriage, and to tell you the truth, I thought it was, too. For her, and perhaps for me, it was like going out on a date. Eventually we had separate bedrooms because she couldn't stand my snoring any longer. Even her earplugs didn't work. At least, that was what she claimed.

"Men and women who share their bedrooms and see each other day in and day out grow bored with each other," she told me. She had read it in one of her romance novels. "The woman, any woman, doesn't like to be caught at her worst moments, and the early hours before makeup and hair are the worst. How is a woman supposed to remain exciting to a man if there are never any surprises anymore?"

She amused me in those days. I laughed and agreed and we set up the separate bedrooms. During the time when I was treating your mother and when we fell in love, that wall between Alberta and myself grew thicker and thicker.

Anyway, she was so angry with me that night, she didn't even come around to tell me all about her event, as she often did. I heard some other doors slammed, and then the house was quiet and I went to bed myself. For a long time I just lay there looking up at the dark ceiling, which occasionally flickered with the starlight that slipped between some clouds. I found myself reviewing your mother's history and realized I had memorized almost all of it, every player, every place, every significant event she had revealed to Dr. Anderson in Palm Beach.

I felt that wave of determination wash over me again. I would bring this woman back to where she could fall in love again, and I would do it, I thought, or rather confessed to myself, because I wanted her to fall in love with me.

Am I shocking you? Your solid-like-a-rock, internationally famous psychiatrist of a father, author, lecturer, consultant, admitting that he had selfish motives? It's true, Willow. It's true.

I went to sleep that night with Grace Montgomery's eyes in mine and her name on my lips.

Alberta was never up before I left for the clinic. Usually she slept until ten or eleven unless she had a lunch appointment. We had hired a maid to cook and take care of all the cleaning in the house, including looking after our clothing, although Miles did most of that for me. At the time I am writing this, your stepmother has hired and fired three maids. We were on our third, Lettia Young, a forty-eight-year-old African-American woman your stepmother hired after a friend of her mother's passed away. I never found much wrong with the previous two, but your stepmother was already complaining about Lettia's cooking, criticizing her for putting in too much salt or too little salt. I suspected Lettia was on the verge of quitting.

She prepared my breakfast. Miles was usually up an hour or so before I was and had already eaten. He waited for me outside as usual and was surprised at how quickly I came out of the house.

"Breakfast is the most important meal of the day," he told me.

"I ate, I ate," I said, but he shook his head skeptically.

Again, an ironic reversal, Willow: my former patient was now looking after me with the concern of a doctor.

"Going to rain a bit today," he said. "Might clear up this afternoon, though."

I looked out the window and just realized how overcast it was. It actually surprised me. The moment I had woken that morning, my eyes seemed filled with sunshine, Willow. I had an energy I hadn't had for some time. I felt like you do when you're about to do something you've never done. You know what I mean, I'm sure: that fresh excitement.

Miles glanced at me a few times in the rearview mirror.

"Going to eat at the clinic again tonight?" he asked.

"Maybe."

He nodded.

"You're working too hard again, Doc," he muttered.

"Those batteries got to be regenerated from time to time," he lectured. "You're the one taught me that, too."

"I know, Miles. I'm fine."

"Do as I teach, not as I do, huh?"

I laughed. Miles had a real down-to-earth view of things. It was refreshing to me even though Alberta thought his words and behavior proved he was capable of becoming mentally disturbed again. She mistook his quiet, methodical manner as mental slowness and absolutely refused to permit him to drive her any-where. It was something for which Miles was grateful.

"It's embarrassing to have an insane person driving our Mercedes, Claude," she would say.

"He isn't an insane person and he never was insane, Alberta. He had a traumatic event in his life, and it drove him into a deep depression. He's fine now," I assured her. She wouldn't accept that.

"I'll be looking into that hot-water heater problem today, Doc," he told me when he pulled up to the clinic. "Return about seven?"

"I'll call you, Miles," I told him and entered the clinic.

Nurse Gordon was there in the lobby speaking to Edith and turned to me the moment I stepped through the door. Except for me and Dr. Price, no one was at the clinic more than Nadine Gordon.

"Your new patient refuses to come out of her room," she said. "I thought you might want to handle it yourself, so I didn't do anything else."

"Yes, you were correct, Ms. Gordon. Thank you. I'll look in on her first thing," I said.

I glanced at Edith and then hurried to the patient housing corridor. Once again, this was in no way a terribly unusual event concerning a new patient or any patient, for that matter. We usually took on only patients who were at least at a basic minimum of normal behavior. They would eat, sleep, participate in some recreation on their own.

I knocked on Grace's door and then stepped into the room. She had the curtains drawn, and as I've already written, it was a rather dark, dismal morning. She was in bed, her blanket drawn to her chin, staring up at the ceiling, not caring about or taking notice of my arrival.

"Good morning, Grace," I said and crossed to the windows to open the curtains and let in whatever light we had. Then I turned on a nightstand lamp. She blinked rapidly before turning toward me. "Still tired?" I asked. "Didn't you sleep well?"

"The pills make me sleep, but I don't have any reason to get up," she said.

"Oh, that's not true, not true at all," I told her and pulled up the desk chair. "You have lots of reason to get up and to get well again."

She raised her eyebrows skeptically.

"You have someone waiting for you at home, someone who needs you and will need you for a long time to come," I said.

"He has my mother," she replied.

"It's not the same thing, Grace. You know that better than I do."

"No, I don't. He's better off with my mother."

"Is he? Do you really think so?"

She turned away.

"I haven't been doing this all that long, but I have had the benefit of so many wise and talented doctors under whom I assisted," I continued softly. "If there is anything that is true about all of us, it's that there is a very, very special relationship between a mother and her child. Nothing can substitute for it, and many of the problems I've seen come about because something happens to that relationship. Both the mother and the child need each other, Grace. It's true for the child and his or her father, of course, but I believe and many of my colleagues believe that because a mother carries her child, there's something a little more involved.

"I'm sure you miss Linden terribly already and that's good, Grace. Don't be afraid to admit to that. That's hopeful," I concluded.

She was blinking away new tears as rapidly as they emerged.

"I can't be any good to him like this and I'll never be better."

"Yes, you will. Sure you will."

"I'm afraid," she said. "Afraid that I will bring him bad luck, too."

"Now there you go saying that again. Okay," I said, sitting back with my arms crossed over my chest, "how was it decided that you should be the one to bring bad luck to people, Grace?"

"I don't know."

"Did you do something terrible before you were born?" I asked.

She looked at me. "Of course not," she said. "How could I?"

"Did you do something terrible when you were younger?"

"No."

"Was your father a bad man?"

"No!" she said emphatically.

"Your mother, she did something terrible?"

"No."

"So why were you chosen? Why are you being punished?"

"I don't know."

"I know many people who have suffered great tragedies in their lives, and many of them were involved with me in one way or another, Grace. Why shouldn't I say I'm bad luck to them? I'm cursed?"

She turned away. "I don't know," she muttered.

"Maybe," I said softly, "you don't know the answer because it's the wrong question. Neither you nor I am bad luck to people. Unfortunate things happen to people. Sometimes it's their own faults; sometimes it is just bad luck, coincidence, whatever, but you can't blame it on yourself, your contact with them, Grace."

She just shook her head.

"You just don't want to come to the realization that bad things can happen to people at any time, for any reason. Life is fragile. None of us likes knowing that, Grace, but your finding fault in yourself doesn't change that."

She looked at me and I smiled.

"I'm just as afraid of life at times as you are, Grace,

but we've got to put it aside if we're to go on and be of any value to anyone, least of all ourselves."

She almost smiled.

"I haven't had breakfast yet," I said. It wasn't entirely a lie. I had only some juice, coffee, and a piece of toast. I was in too much of a hurry to get here. "Get yourself up and dressed and we'll have it together."

"Don't you have other patients to attend to?" she asked with some suspicion. Was I spending so much time with her because she was so ill? she probably wondered.

"Oh, certainly, but I can't work on an empty stomach, now can I?" I asked her and she gave in to a small smile. "I'm going to my office to check on my messages and such. I'll meet you in the dining room, okay?"

I reached out and touched her arm.

"Okay?"

She nodded.

"Good," I said, rising. "Sorry the weather is so poor today. I was going to suggest we go for a walk. Maybe it will clear up later. My driver Miles thinks it might."

"A walk?"

"Sure. Wait until you see our gardens," I told her.

She shook her head, a look of confusion sitting on her face.

"What's wrong?" I asked.

"This doesn't feel like . . ."

"Like what?"

"A place for crazy people," she said.

"It isn't," I told her. "It's a place for people who want to be happy only. That's why I spend so much time here," I told her, and she widened her smile.

What a beautiful smile, I thought. I felt like an artist repairing a great painting.

You see, Willow, I think I was already too far gone as a man to forget it and be only her doctor.

# 4

# The Sound of Her Laughter

Willow, I'm sure you are probably asking yourself how do I remember these conversations with your mother in such great detail.

My conversations with patients comprise the spine of my efforts to help them. Their words are the main source of revelations about their inner selves. Their actions or lack of actions are the reasons why they are brought here, of course, but the cause of those actions and inactions, what gives birth to them, that takes deep digging, Willow, and my principal tool is my questioning and their responses. I'm trained to remember what they say as it is, but with my added emotional involvement, I found Grace's words carving themselves not only in my mind, but in my heart as well. I don't know if you will have fallen in love by the time you read this, but if you have, you will understand.

We took our walk after breakfast. Before that, I conferred with Dr. Price and asked him to pick up two of my other patients who had sessions scheduled with me that day so I could shift my efforts and give Grace Montgomery more time. One of them was Sandy.

Ralston Price and I have been together ever since medical school. I have had and have at this moment no closer associate. When two people have gone through as much as Ralston Price and I have together, we can read each other almost as well as we can read ourselves. Up until this occasion, there were few secrets between us. For example, Ralston knew how my relationship with Alberta had changed, or should I say, drifted into something much less than it ever was. The truth was he was never fond of her and she was definitely never fond of him. She once told me his eyes were too close together, and her grandmother had drilled it into her head that a man with close eyes was sneaky and never to be trusted. I actually pulled out pictures of great men in history to illustrate how foolish that superstition was, but when Alberta formed an idea, it was formed in stone and rolled around in her mind forever.

After I made my request, Ralston raised his somewhat bushy light brown eyebrows and relaxed his lips into that somewhat impish smile of his.

"What is the reason for this intense approach, Claude?" he asked. "And with a patient you have hardly met?"

"I think I can make significant progress in a short

period. She's reachable," I said. "It's more of a case of having someone she trusts. She's already quite forth-coming."

His head moved in a slow tilt to the right as his skepticism fattened and fattened right before my eyes.

"I see, and you were able to make this analysis in one day?" he asked, one eyebrow higher than the other.

"Yes, I was," I said. "And she has a little boy wait-ing for her at home," I practically shouted at him.

He pressed his lips together and uttered that famous "Ummm" of his. Then he flipped the pages of his cal-endar and nodded. "Okay, Claude. Let's see how it goes for a while. I'll take on those other patients for you."

"Thank you, Ralston."

I started out of his office and he said, "Claude." I turned. "Don't reach too high. Remember our wings of wax," he reminded me. I nodded.

He was referring to that myth of Icarus, the boy who, with his inventive father, tried to escape an island imprisonment with wings attached by wax. He was warned not to fly too closely to the sun or the wings would melt. We psychiatrists like to use it to illustrate how arrogance can be your downfall.

Like Icarus, I was not to listen to the warning, but this was a happy fall, Willow. Without it, you wouldn't have been born and I wouldn't have known true love. I'd gladly fly too close to the sun repeatedly if it meant I'd have you and Grace's love again and again and again.

After breakfast, as I had suggested, Grace and I

took that walk. I found that when one of my patients reached the point where he or she could be comfortable outside my office, I would try to get him or her to take one of my famous walks. Somehow, without spending much time with her, I knew Grace would be more comfortable. She was curious, however, even suspicious about this almost immediately.

"Dr. Anderson never spoke with me out of his office," she said. "Even if he saw me somewhere else, which was not often, he would barely say hello, especially if I was with my mother. She didn't want anyone to know I was seeing him."

"I'll tell you a secret, Grace. I make it seem as if we're just going on a walk, but it's way more than that. I try to sneak up on my patients and doing things that are a bit unorthodox helps."

She liked that. She enjoyed my honesty. With her head slightly lowered, but holding on to that soft Mona Lisa–like smile on her lips, she walked along. I confess I couldn't take my eyes off her, Willow, and no matter how twisted and troubled she was inside herself, I sensed that she knew I couldn't. We doctors, especially we psychiatrists, like to pride ourselves on our stoical expression, what you called my doctor mask, and I know I rarely, if ever, unmasked myself, but with your mother, right from that first day, it was as if my doctor mask was made of a thin layer of ice and either melted in the presence of her beauty or slipped off.

As we walked, I asked her about her youth, prodded deeper and deeper into the origin of these terrible fears that plagued her. I quickly understood that even as a little girl she was worried about her father, worried that when he went away, he would never come back. It made every return special, wonderful. It wasn't hard to see that these sort of emotional ups and downs took its toll on an impressionable child.

However, every time her father returned, her confidence in him grew.

"I thought Daddy was indestructible," she admitted. We were sitting on a bench by now, looking out over the field and hills behind the clinic. The threat of rain had passed, and as Miles had predicted, the gray overcast sky was shattering like brittle china, slices of sunlight forming a web of promise behind them.

"He was so strong," she said, "so tall and handsome and confident, and I saw how other men looked up to him and saluted him and snapped to attention when he appeared. How could he die? How could he not come back to me?"

"And so you thought if that could happen to him, it could happen to anyone. In fact, you expected it to happen to everyone you loved, didn't you, Grace?"

"Yes," she said, her eyes widening a little. She nodded. "Yes."

"People like to say the only thing certain to expect is death and taxes. None of us has any more assurances than that, Grace. You can't predict much more and definitely not someone else's future. Here I am a psychiatrist. I'm supposed to know how to read people's minds and anticipate what they will do, but it's not an exact science. Actually, that's what makes people interesting to me."

"What?" she asked me.

Our eyes locked.

"That they are unpredictable, that even a man like I am might do and think unexpected things, might do something out of character."

She held my gaze a moment longer and then looked down.

"You put too much on yourself, Grace," I said. "Those pretty shoulders shouldn't have to carry that much weight, carry other people's futures and fate. Not that I couldn't see why someone, some man might want to trust you with all that."

She didn't look at me, but I could see just a slight tint of crimson rise to the surface of her cheeks.

"I read about all the people you thought you somehow injured just by being close to them. Every one of them had his own history, Grace. Every one of them made decisions without you present and all had done significant things before they even knew you. Many of the things they already had done influenced what eventually happened to them. Please consider that whenever you think to blame yourself."

She almost nodded.

"Dr. Anderson said similar things to me," she told me.

"Well, he wasn't wrong, Grace."

"Somehow," she said, turning to me, "it didn't sound as convincing as when you say it."

I smiled. "I told you it's more effective to do unorthodox things with your patients."

Her smiled widened.

"If you're up to it," I said, "I'd like to show you the view from that rise there." I nodded toward the hill about a thousand yards or so ahead of us. "It's quite beautiful."

"Sneaking up on me again, Dr. De Beers?" she asked and I laughed. Then she looked out toward the hill, and after a long moment of decision, as if this one would change her life somehow, she said, "Okay."

Sometimes, Willow, your mother's voice sounded like the voice of a little girl. She retreated to that innocent vulnerable state, and when she did, my heart went out even more to her. It took all my professional bearing to keep from putting my arm around her and pressing her to me. I so wanted to kiss that cheek, to touch her hair, to trace the perfect lines of her perfect lips, but I shut all that up in the deepest place in my mind and rose from the bench we were on to walk again. She kept her arms crossed under her breasts, her head slightly lowered, her eyes more thoughtful now.

I am writing this just after your tenth birthday, Willow, so I don't know how often you might have visited me at my clinic before you actually read this, but I do know that when you are old enough, I will take you for the same walk I took your mother that day. I might have the courage to reveal everything to you then, and if I do, there would be little reason to have my attorney give this to you.

As you know, we have some beautiful grounds at our home, but because of the hills here at the clinic, I have this wonderful view to share with my patients. From the crest I brought your mother to, we could see the river snaking along, its surface now gleaming with an opalescence in the strengthening late morning sunlight.

"My mother used to tell me rivers are the circulatory system for the earth, carrying the earth's blood: water. She was a very intelligent, well-read woman and she had a big influence on me and my success in science," I said. "It was like having a home study program."

I remember thinking I never talked about my personal life like this with any of my patients, but every time I did, it brought a new smile to Grace's lips. Was I doing it just to win her trust, something a doctor needs to help his patient, or was I doing it because it felt good to speak about myself whenever I was with her, because it was something special?

"I read where you wanted to become a teacher. Do you still want to do that?" I asked her.

She looked at me, and I could see the idea of her ever becoming or doing anything with her life anymore seemed incredible.

"I don't know," she said timidly, as someone afraid to have any hope would.

I was angry, angry at all the events, the people, the forces that had turned this remarkable, beautiful, promising young woman into an unconfident, weak shadow of what she had every right to be.

"Now, you listen to me," I said, seizing her just below the elbow and stopping her on the path. "You're going to have a future, Grace Montgomery. You're not going to be here or in the care of doctors forever," I said with steely eyes of determination.

"What makes you so certain of that?" she asked, obviously impressed with my firmness.

"Experience, years of study, and . . ."

"And what?"

"Faith," I said. "Faith in you, Grace."

"But you hardly know me. You're read the file Dr. Anderson sent to you, but that's not me."

"I know it's not."

"Then how do you have any faith in me?"

"Maybe it's the faith I have in myself," I said, trying not to sound too arrogant.

"You're not what I expected," she said again after a long moment, and this time we both laughed.

Oh, Willow, the sound of her laughter . . . it was truly music, a free and melodic song. It had been so long since I shared such a happy, carefree moment with anyone. I felt a little liberated myself. Suddenly it was brighter than I had thought. Those clouds were fleeing. The sun was making every color more vibrant, the very air we breathed was sweeter.

I wondered to myself, *Is this what is meant by falling in love?* As a psychiatrist, I often had trouble with such romantic concepts. Nothing in the world seemed magical to me before I met your mother, Willow. Everything had an explanation either at the bottom of good scientific analysis or in its very physical qualities.

We were living in a world in which more and more accurate prognosticators were designed and created to predict what people would do, how they would vote, what they would buy, and even, in some people's way of thinking, whom they would love. I was part of that world, one of those prognosticators. If anyone should be skeptical of magic, it was I, Willow, but I loved the possibility that there was magic in the world, that there were things that we were incapable of anticipating.

I couldn't remember enjoying a session with any patient as much as I was enjoying this walk with your mother. I wished it would go on and on and even considered walking with her down to the river's edge. I was invigorated. I felt gigantic. I could cure her in one session. Ralston would be waving his finger at me, I thought, but I didn't have a chance to do any of that on our second day.

"Dr. De Beers!" we heard someone shouting. I turned and saw Nurse Gordon hurrying toward us. "Come quickly!" she cried, gesturing.

"Let's hurry back, Grace," I said.

"What's happening? What's wrong?" I asked as we drew closer to Nadine Gordon.

"Sandy," she said. "She's jabbed a fork into her stomach! She's in the infirmary." She looked at Grace and then turned back to me. "She was supposed to be with you this hour."

"Dr. Price was going to see her," I said. "Didn't you get the new orders?"

"No. I was involved in another situation with the Masterson boy. He was having one of his tantrums in the recreation room and your young doctor Wheeler was overwhelmed," she shot back at me and started for the clinic.

I hurried after her and told Grace to try to relax, go

to the arts and crafts room, perhaps. She nodded and
went off while I hurried to the infirmary, where I
found Ralston conferring with Thomas Wheeler, the
young doctor.

"What happened?"

"Hallucinating again. She believed one of the dark
figures got into her and she was digging it out."

"How terrible," I said.

"An inch or so to the right and she might have bled
to death," Ralston told me. "I thought Nadine Gordon
was bringing her to my office, and I got distracted during a phone call and didn't notice the time."

"I did leave written instructions for Nurse Gordon
to take her to see you," I said. "She's usually right on
that, but she said she had some difficulties in the recreation room with Billy Masterson?"

"Yes, he was acting out," Dr. Wheeler said. "But I
was handling it just fine," he added defensively. "She
could have attended to her own duties, especially if
she had some orders from you to follow."

Ralston leaned toward me to whisper, "You should
have given her the orders orally, Claude."

"Yes," I said, now feeling terrible. *This is not something I would have done before,* I told myself. *I'm too
distracted.*

"All right, Dr. Wheeler," Ralston told him. "Let's
get back to our schedule. Things are under control."

He nodded and left us.

"Where were you anyway, Claude?" Ralston asked
me.

"I took Grace Montgomery for a walk. She was a

great deal more at ease out there. I was making good progress with her."

"Ummm. Okay, let's check on Sandy and get back to our other patients," he added.

I didn't see your mother again until the end of the day. She had spent a good part of her afternoon in the arts and crafts room. We had a former art teacher working for us, Joan Richards. She was very good with the patients and often joked that she saw little difference between her working with mentally disabled people and teenagers. Grace took to her quickly and had already begun work on creating a doll.

It wasn't hard to analyze that, Willow. Your mother was recreating Linden, her own baby. Nothing underlined her need to be with her child as much. In subsequent sessions with her I would come to understand that Grace resented her mother's assuming her role. She was even bitter about it at times. I encouraged her to express that. From a psychiatric point of view, it's good to get the patient to let it all out, so to speak, to get her to bring her darkest, most troubling thoughts up from the depths of her turmoil and express it. Once she does, it's the beginning of her ability to deal with it and overcome the problems. (This sounds like it comes from a manual on psychiatry, I know, but I have a suspicion that by the time you read this, you will appreciate the occasional comments.)

"My mother tells me she did it and is doing it for my own good," Grace revealed through clenched teeth one day when we began to talk in earnest about this problem.

"Don't you believe her?" I asked.

"No."

"Why not?"

"She knows I never cared about what those people thought of me." Then she looked up at me and said, "She and my father were going to have another child, you know."

It wasn't something she had told Dr. Anderson, so I considered it something of a breakthrough.

"Why didn't they?"

"He was killed before they could, but she came to me one day and told me that now that he was stationed for a long period of time in one place, and now that he had been given a higher rank with a better salary, they felt more relaxed and confident and decided to try. She had tried before but had not become pregnant, and she blamed it on her stress and nervousness. At least, her doctors told her that. I remember her telling me how she and my father had gone to doctors to be sure that she could become pregnant."

"So you think that because of that . . ."

"Linden was the child she never could have, the child she wanted," she asserted. "I was almost the surrogate mother, not her."

"How do you mean?"

"You know, like those women who carry another woman's fertilized egg in their wombs."

I thought this analysis of her mother and herself was quite perceptive of her, and my appreciation of her rose even higher, as well as my expectations for a complete recovery.

"How do you think you should deal with this, Grace?" I asked her.

She thought a long moment.

"I've got to get stronger," she concluded. "I've got to go home and take my baby back."

"That's right," I said. "That's exactly what you have to do, Grace."

She looked up at me and we just stared at each other for the longest moment. It took all my professionalism, all my psychiatric skill to keep me seated in that chair, Willow. The man inside me was practically screaming for me to get up and go to her and put my hands on her arms and stand her up so I could kiss her and hold her and tell her the secrets of my own heart, but I managed to shut him down. I pretended to make notes, think, and then told her we had done enough. We had made some wonderful progress.

"You are getting stronger, Grace," I added. "We can adjust your medications accordingly."

She liked that.

"Thanks to you," she said. "And your sneaky ways."

I'm sure I had my best Christmas smile on my lips, the most joyful, giving smile I could manage. How delightful she could be, Willow. I never had a patient with so much personality. My reactions to her weren't programmed, weren't designed just to make her more comfortable. They were sincere reactions, and she knew it just as much as I did.

*This secret you're holding inside you, Claude De Beers,* I told myself, *it can't be hidden forever.*

And it would not be.

# 5

# A Pure and Wonderful Love

Like anyone with guilt in his heart, I couldn't help wondering just how much Alberta sensed when she looked at me and spoke to me during those early months when I was treating your mother, Willow. Ironically, I became grateful for all Alberta's distractions. Perhaps it was solely because of them that she was unable to take one look at me and see how lovesick I had become. I could not imagine how she missed it. Whenever I stopped for a moment in my home and gazed at myself in the mirror, I saw a different Claude De Beers, one who barely resembled the man everyone knew as Dr. De Beers, the renowned psychiatrist, lecturer, author, the mature, confident man of logic and reason, unflappable.

How could even Alberta be so oblivious to my long

pauses during our conversations, my daydreaming, my drifting through our home, walking like a ghost on air, being forgetful, even to the point of having to be reminded about dinner. One morning I was in such haste to get to the clinic, I even forgot my tie and Miles had to remind me. Fortunately, I had one in the car at all times.

And at our dinners whenever we did eat together and Alberta went on and on about her activities or things she wanted us to buy or change in the house, how could she not notice my blank stare, my failure to comment, to question, to respond to anything, to give her my usual nod or simple yes and no? Why didn't she see how I nibbled at my food?

Was all this in my imagination? Was I merely lost in some fantasy? Would it all come to an abrupt end? Shouldn't I want it to come to an abrupt end? I asked myself.

I was caught in a great conflict, you see. On the one hand, I was doing all in my power to help Grace regain enough self-confidence to throw off the demons that had brought her here, and on the other, I was secretly hoping she would never leave, that we would go on forever, walking, talking, catching each other's longing in each other's eyes, and eventually. . . .

Eventually what?

*What do you expect will happen, Claude De Beers?* I asked myself each day I headed for the clinic. *Can't you see how impossible all this is? You can only ruin someone else's life along with your own.* The voice of my conscience grew louder and stronger almost every new day. One night I arrived at what I thought was a prescription for ending all this. I decided to throw myself at Alberta, to try to resurrect our early passion for each other, to cure myself of this nonsense by reminding myself in no uncertain terms that I was a married man.

It was a good night to try it. Alberta had not gone to any of her usual meetings, lunches, or dinners. She had spent the day meeting with some decorators because she wanted to redo our sitting room and our entryway. The house was old, but historic, a classic structure in our community. She knew I would not permit her to change the exterior very much, so she focused her attention on modernizing the interior. I used to think our furniture should be on wheels. She had it moved around and changed that often. Every time she visited one of her wealthy friends, she returned depressed about our home. For Alberta, the grass would always be greener somewhere else.

I confess I was somewhat to blame for her behavior. As long as she was doing these things, she wasn't nagging me, criticizing me for the time I spent at my clinic. Occasionally she would burst into my office with a brochure of furnishings or with samples of rugs and demand I give her an opinion.

"Well, which is right for the room?" she would ask again, impatient with the time I was taking.

Almost invariably, what I chose, she hated. I began to think that my not choosing what she liked was her way of confirming her choice was correct. In her mind I had no taste, no sense of style because I was the classic absentminded professor. It was all simply another nail in the coffin that marked the death of our marriage, and I have to admit that after I had met Grace Montgomery, I not only didn't notice all the nails. I didn't care.

It frightened me. Would I, the psychiatrist's psychiatrist, go mad myself?

*Bring it to an end,* I ordered my rebellious heart. *Bring this all to an abrupt and final end. And there is no better way to do that than to reinforce the oath of marriage you have already taken,* I told myself.

I fortified myself with a tumbler of scotch on the rocks and concentrated my thoughts on memories of Alberta when we had first met, courted, and made love. I blamed my infatuation with Grace and my own neglectful ways on my failure to regenerate my own marriage. I had become too comfortable with myself and my work, and now I was almost a married man living like a bachelor. Why should I blame Alberta for her interest in other things? What had I done to deserve her romantic interest in me? I was rarely escorting her to social events anymore. We had so little in common, and that was at least half my fault, I told myself. I had to do something to change that.

In short, I was fleeing from Grace, retreating to my own marriage.

Would it work?

I knocked on Alberta's bedroom door.

"Yes?" she called.

"It's Claude," I said. "May I come in?"

She opened the door and looked out at me. She

was in her nightgown and had her hair in a hair net. I
could see she had just begun to remove her makeup.
She looked a little annoyed until she saw the tumbler
of scotch in my hand. I hadn't realized I was still carrying it.

"What is it, Claude?" she asked with a curious little
smile nesting on her lips.

"I was wondering if I could stop in to see you," I
said.

Our long love droughts and lack of intimacy made
me sound more formal than I wanted to be.

"Why?" she asked.

There was a time when she wouldn't have had to
ask that, I thought, although it was never easy for me
to be amorous. Perhaps that was why I was so eager
and happy to marry Alberta. Here was a very attractive
young woman with a certain elegance who was willing to accept me as I was, at least in the beginning. I
was quite conscious of my male friends and associates
thinking I had done the equivalent of winning the lot-
tery. Why would such a stunning beauty want to be
with me above anyone else? Not that I think of myself
as an unattractive man. Hardly that, Willow. I am just
realistic about my romantic qualities and admit I am
and was not the most exciting beau she could find or
even the most exciting she was courting. I am quite
familiar with the Don Juan syndrome, but I am by no
means a Don Juan.

In any case I felt a bit awkward standing there with
a drink in my hand that was obviously needed to bol-
ster my courage.

"Well, I just . . . thought . . . it's been a while since . . . I mean . . ."

"Really? What did you do, Claude, get yourself a testosterone booster?" she asked dryly.

I guess my face fell a bit.

She shook her head and stepped back.

"Come in," she said. "I don't see you drinking much anymore or relaxing in any way," she added, nodding at the glass in my hand.

"Yes, I know. I've been so occupied with my work, I . . ."

"Forgot you were married? I know," she said and laughed. She removed her hair net and shook out her hair a bit. "You're lucky," she said. "Twenty minutes more and you would have been out of luck. I would have my facial set, and I don't think that would have been very attractive to you. Loosen your tie, at least, Claude. You look as if you're here to give me therapy," she added and laughed again.

I smiled.

I suppose I was a funny sight standing there in my jacket and tie, my drink in hand, looking more like a meek librarian asking someone to please pay her library debt.

As she spoke to me, Alberta looked at herself in the mirror and primped her hair.

"The first time you and I made love, I thought you were following some sex how-to book. You kept asking me, "Is that all right? Is this all right? It was more like an examination than lovemaking, Claude."

"I'm sorry," I said.

"Since then I've taught you a lot and you've become better at it. It's funny that I had to teach a psychiatrist the art of making love, don't you think? You, of all people, should know how important the fantasy is. That's why I have worked so hard to make this room so plush and feminine," she said, gesturing at the velvet drapes, the canopy bed, the gilded mirrors, and the plush carpeting. "I don't know if you even notice what an effort I make. Do you, Claude?"

"Of course I notice. It's a beautiful room. You have done wonders with it," I told her, gazing around and nodding as if it were really the first time I had seen it.

"I'll say I have. I've done wonders with this whole house. Your mother lived as if she didn't have a penny. Some of the things in this house were literally rotting away when I first came here to live with you, Claude. I was surprised your father didn't have more pride in his home. He did have people visiting often, didn't he?"

"Oh, yes."

"They must have been very disappointed with what they found. Now, at least, this is the home of a successful doctor and we don't have to be embarrassed. I wouldn't have it look any less, but do you appreciate that?"

"I do, Alberta. I might not show it because I'm so involved in my work, but I do," I protested.

She smirked. "It's all right if you don't. I appreciate enough for the both of us," she said. "So"—she continued turning to me and undoing her nightgown, "you remembered you were married to an attractive woman and the man in you was finally stirred up, is that it?"

"No, I . . . I mean, yes, I mean . . ."

"Forget about it. I'm not looking for a scientific explanation. Are you going to get undressed, Claude, or do you expect me to do that for you?" she asked.

I looked about to place my drink on something, and she screamed, "Not there. Put it on the desk. You'll leave a circle in the wood. How you can be so intelligent and do so many stupid things, I don't know."

I put the glass down where she wanted it put and began to undress.

No matter what, I thought, it just wasn't romantic. It just wasn't emanating from any heart beating with love, and the irony was, it was she who was always teaching, instructing, critiquing it all, not me. She was analyzing, comparing, designing every movement to fit some preconceived image. She put herself in a romance novel or a movie love scene, and I was the one who was no more than a prop, a manikin standing in for this actor or that dreamboat.

I won't go into all that happened afterward, Willow, but I can tell you this—when I lay back on my own pillow in my own bed afterward that night, I was even more in love with Grace. How do I know? I couldn't make love to Alberta without thinking about Grace, without doing just what Alberta did most likely every time we were together: pretending she was with someone else. In my case it wasn't a movie actor or a singing star I was imagining, nor was it a debonair socialite. It was someone I knew, someone I could touch.

*Grace,* I kept thinking in my mind, *Grace, how I*

*want to curl up in your heart and sleep contented for-
ever and ever. How can that ever be?* Just thinking
such thoughts made me ashamed of myself. Grace
Montgomery was my patient. It was assumed she was
vulnerable and in my most protected trust. A doctor
cannot take advantage of that trust, can he? He can't
and remain true to his profession, to the essence of
who and what he is and abuse that relationship.

I tossed and turned, trying to keep myself from
dreaming of her. I deliberately reviewed my reports on
other patients. I planned my whole month's calendar. I
did everything I could to keep awake, for fear that
once I fell asleep, I would fall victim to my own secret
heart, which, my darling Willow, was exactly what did
happen.

Over the next few days I kept my sessions with
Grace as professional as I could. I met with her only in
my office, and I spent time working on correcting her
medications. I busied myself with my other patients,
and I tried desperately to occupy my every free hour
with something that would keep me from thinking
about her. Nothing worked.

*This is madness,* I kept telling myself. *I'm growing
more and more obsessed.* It had to stop, but for all my
wisdom and for all my experience, I could not heal
myself, Willow. I could not purge my mind of your
mother. Her eyes, her lips, her hair, the way she held
her head or moved her hands, every little thing about
her was caught in a mental snapshot and replayed on
the screen of my memory and in the corridors of my
dreams.

Finally one night after I had finished dinner and Alberta had gone upstairs, I went to my office and tried to reason with myself. I reviewed my thoughts, my actions. What should I do next to stop this fall into a sweet oblivion? I had another tumbler of scotch and then went up to bed, but almost as soon as my head hit the pillow, your mother's face returned to the inside of my eyelids.

In a crazed rush of impulsive activity, I rose, dressed, and left the house. Miles was already asleep. I drove myself back to the clinic. It was a very dark night, overcast, with not a star in sight. The clinic looked asleep itself, the lights turned down low and the lobby very quiet. All of our patients were in their rooms, and the attendants and nurses were sitting and having coffee or tea or watching television. I was able to let myself in and, like some burglar, sneak down the corridor. When I reached Grace Montgomery's door, I stopped and stood there, my heart pounding.

What was I doing?

Why had I come here?

What were my intentions?

I saw my hand move slowly toward the doorknob, and then I heard, "Dr. De Beers?"

One of the night nurses had appeared in the corridor.

"Oh, Suzanne," I said.

"Is anything wrong?"

"I was a little concerned about Grace Montgomery today and wanted to check on her. How has she been?"

"Fine," she said, shaking her head. "Nothing out of

the ordinary. She ate well, worked in the arts and crafts room, did some reading in our library. I'm sure she's asleep."

"Yes, yes, you're probably right," I said.

"But let me look in on her for you," she added and opened the door.

I peered in over her shoulder like a voyeur, a child wanting to see something exciting. Grace was asleep, her face caught in the moonlight peeking through her curtains. She looked absolutely angelic to me.

"She's fine, Doctor," the nurse said. I nodded and we both backed out and closed the door softly.

*I am truly a madman,* I thought on the way home that night. *Tomorrow, tomorrow I will turn her over completely to Ralston.*

But when I arrived at the clinic the next morning and went to his office to do just that, I found I couldn't even suggest it. Not yet. I wasn't ready for such surrender. I had to continue to test myself, and perhaps, dear Willow, perhaps that was where I went right. You would have expected me to say wrong, but even to this day I refuse to believe I was guilty of anything but a pure and wonderful love.

We returned to our walks, our wonderful walks. Grace was talking more and more about her life in Palm Beach now, telling me how difficult it had been for her to make new friends and how out of place she had felt right from the beginning.

"I had come from a very structured world, the world of a navy family on a navy base, and was dropped into this . . . this world where rules almost didn't matter, Doctor. My new friends didn't worry much about disappointing their parents. I used to think some of them actually didn't like their own parents."

"Yes, that's not something that surprises me. Young people want to have some structure. You might think otherwise, but when they're tossed out to sink or swim on their own, they feel neglected and should feel that way. Disciplining, supervising is another way to show you care."

"Were your parents that way?"

"Oh, yes," I said, laughing. "My father was a very strict disciplinarian, not that I really needed it. I was too well behaved and responsible. I was probably very boring to my classmates, a bookworm. Even as a teenager, I hated wasting time."

"Didn't you have girlfriends?" she asked. "Didn't you fall in love a dozen times?"

"I had crushes on girls in my classes, but I was always a bit too shy to make anything of it."

"Your wife is very attractive. You couldn't be all that shy," she said.

I began to wonder if someone who didn't know listened in, who would he think was the patient here? It made me smile.

"Why are you laughing?" she wondered.

"I'm not laughing at you. I'm laughing at the contradiction. Yes, my wife is beautiful, but if you asked me what was it about me that drew her attention, I think I would have a hard time giving you a satisfactory answer."

"Oh, I think I know that answer," Grace said.

We were on the crest of that hill, gazing down at the river again.

"Really?" I smiled at her. "What's the answer?"

"You make people feel comfortable with themselves. You're like a warm home. I feel like I could cuddle up and go to sleep safely in your arms, and I haven't felt that way since . . . since my father died," she said.

For a long moment, Willow, I just stood there. Yes, your literate, wordy father was speechless and brought to that point by this purely innocent beautiful woman whose eyes untied the last cords that bound me to my oaths, my profession, my responsibilities. I reached out and put my hand on her shoulder and slowly, ever so slowly, brought her closer until I was holding her against me.

Neither of us spoke, but it was a moment I can't forget. We did nothing more than stand there looking out at the river, watching the gauze-like layer of clouds slide gracefully down the blue slope of sky toward the horizon. A flock of sparrows lifted from the branch of a tree below and flew to the right until they disappeared behind the forest. And then the world seemed to take a deep breath. The breeze stopped. The strands of her hair that were lifted fell back to her forehead.

"Are you happy now, Doctor, happy with your marriage?" she asked.

Everything in me told me this was not a question I should answer. She was my patient. I was her doctor. This was crossing the line too far.

"It's more of an arrangement than a marriage," I admitted. "As the famous line goes, we share coffee."

It wasn't hard to see that she was pleased with that reply. She said nothing. She nodded softly as if she had expected no other kind of reply.

I lifted my hand from her shoulder and turned, and we walked back to the clinic, neither of us speaking. She returned to the arts and crafts room, and I went to my office to make some notes and prepare myself for my next patient. In the afternoon we had a staff meeting and reviewed our patient load. When Grace Montgomery's name came up, Ralston lifted that one eyebrow of his and listened to my quick evaluation and my recommendations for continued therapies. I was reducing her medication dramatically now. She hadn't been suffering the long bouts of depression she experienced when she had first arrived.

"So you're really making significant progress, Claude," Ralston said.

"Yes, yes I think we are."

"Good." Mercifully he went on to another patient, and I returned to my office. At the end of the day I considered remaining to have dinner with Grace, but I battled with myself and defeated that part of me that wanted it so very much.

At home Alberta was her talkative self, rambling on and on about the chamber of commerce ball. She was insistent that I attend it and drew repeated promises from me that I would not forget nor make any other appointment for that date. She actually had me sign a paper that stated, *I, Claude De Beers, will attend the chamber of commerce ball on _____.*

"I will show this to everyone and anyone should you not be at my side that evening, Claude," she threatened. "The whole world will know what an absolute cad you are."

How trivial and silly it all seemed to me to be at her side at such an event compared to being at Grace's side, even to take a simple walk in the gardens at the clinic.

Later in the evening I tried to do some reading. Alberta had retired to take a herbal bath and do her skin and hair treatments. My eyes kept slipping from the pages of what I was reading until I looked up at the wall and saw Grace Montgomery and myself standing on the hill, me holding her, her head against my chest.

*Are you happy now, Doctor, happy in your marriage?* I heard her ask me again.

How my heart ached, Willow. I could not stand it any longer. I rose and looked for Miles. He was outside, finishing washing the car.

"I need to return to the clinic, Miles," I said.

"Now?"

"Immediately."

He nodded, put everything away quickly, and got behind the wheel. Moments later we were flying through the night, my heart thumping. I had no idea what I would do, what I would say, but I felt wonderful doing this.

"Should I wait for you, Doctor?" Miles asked when we pulled up.

"Yes, Miles," I said. "You can go to the recreation room and watch television if you like."

"Very good," he said and I hurried in.

Nadine Gordon was on duty this night and she saw me enter.

"Is anything wrong, Dr. De Beers?" she asked immediately.

"No, no. I have something to complete. Go on with your usual duties," I said, waving her off as officially and firmly as I could.

I could feel her eyes on the back of my head as I charged down the corridor, first to my office and then, quietly, to the patients' dormitory. Once again, sneaking about like a errant teenager, I approached Grace's door. I knocked softly and then opened it.

She was standing by the window looking out and turned slowly when I appeared. I closed the door softly behind me. She gazed at me without speaking. She was in her nightgown, her hair down. Willow, it was as if I were truly under a spell. I think I floated across that small room until I was inches from her. Neither of us had uttered a syllable yet. She looked up at me, that small, precious smile forming on her lips.

"Grace," I finally found the strength to say, and then, Claude De Beers be damned, I did it, Willow.

I kissed her, tentatively at first and then with more passion than I ever imagined I had within me.

And she kissed me back and held on to me like a castaway bobbing in that sea of turmoil who had found something solid to cling to.

"I'm here," I said. "For you."

And it began.

# 6

# Cain's Confession

$A$ brilliant colleague of mine, another well-known psychiatrist and philosopher who is the author of many of the classic works in our field, has written that the criminal or the immoral person ironically finds relief in the so-called criminal or immoral act. Up until the time he or she commits it, their consciences torment them. They struggle and do battle with good and evil forces within themselves and in that they suffer. When they finally act, they end the discussion. It's over. They've committed themselves and there is, according to my colleague, great relief. He calls it Cain's Confession syndrome. It's equivalent to shouting at his conscience, "I did it! Stop haunting me!"

Oh, did I do it, Willow. I began a secret relationship that would make me deceitful and conniving, a liar in my own house and dishonest with my closest friend, for I could not in the beginning trust anyone with the truth, not even Ralston. I had just come to the point where I was able to trust myself with it.

"I could hurt you," Grace told me that night. Of course she was referring to her curse.

I laughed and told her, "Not any more than I could hurt myself or more to the point, hurt you, Grace."

She trembled in my arms, and I held her and kissed her again and then gently led her to her bed, where she lay back on the pillow and looked up at me with that wonderful soft smile that melted any resistance in my heart. I knelt at her side and stroked her hair.

"This is so wrong of me," I told her. "I am a man of logic, but I cannot explain, much less justify, my actions. All I know is you rarely leave my thoughts. I see you everywhere, Grace. I hear your voice in every quiet moment, and even when others are speaking to me, my ears shut down and your voice is the one I hear. I, of all people, know what obsessions are. This is not simply some obsession, Grace, something that might be mitigated or cured. It's more. I feel certain of that. For the first time, I think I understand the power of love, for I am in love, and Grace, no one can cure me of that or lessen it because I want it with all my soul."

"Except for my father, no man has ever told me he loves me, not like that," she said. "My stepfather Winston was very, very fond of me, but it was truly a father-daughter affection. Until now I never knew love like the love I feel for you." She laughed. "I was going to say Doctor. What should I call you?"

"Call me Claude, of course," I said, smiling. I couldn't stop petting her and bringing my lips to her cheeks, her eyes, her lips.

"I won't call you that unless we're alone," she said.

"This complicates everything, Grace. I promise you that if I come to believe it will hurt you, I will not be your therapist any longer. Promise me you will understand. Please," I begged her.

She promised, but it was one of those promises both people knew was impossible to keep. They make it just to get temporary peace.

I remained beside her, speaking softly to her, kissing her but doing no more. Finally I told her good night.

"Now I know I can sleep," I said. "I'm not keeping it all bottled up inside me. I have followed the advice I give to my patients."

She said nothing. I was afraid I had overwhelmed her. After I slipped out of her room, I started quickly down the corridor. Nadine Gordon stepped out of Sandy's room just as I had passed it and called to me. When I turned, she approached, her forehead creased as she brought her eyebrows together with her puzzled look.

"I looked everywhere for you, Dr. De Beers. Is everything all right?"

"Yes, Ms. Gordon. Everything is all right. How is Sandy?"

"She's sleeping better, but that is about all the improvement I've noticed," she replied curtly. "I think she might require more of your time, Doctor. Perhaps it was not so wise to reassign her to Dr. Price."

"I think he and I will be the best judges of that, Nadine," I said. Whenever she did get to me, annoy me, or displease me in any way, I referred to her by her first name. It was something I know wasn't lost on her.

"Of course. I'm just giving you my most professional opinion, but only to assist you, Doctor, and certainly not to be critical," she added.

I could never tell if Nadine Gordon liked me or disliked me during those earlier days. Sometimes I could actually feel her critical eyes looking over my shoulders, even when she wasn't in the room. No one lived more by the book than she did. I often would wonder what her personal life was like. To me she didn't seem to have any. All I knew was she lived in a single bedroom apartment, had no family in the state, and was unmarried with no prospects lurking in the wings.

She did little to make herself attractive on the job. Her hair was always severely tied back to the point where her skin looked stretched. She had faint freckles over her forehead and very tiny patches of them along her temples with a few dripping down to the crests of her cheeks. Her hair was a shade darker than rust, and her lips were more toward orange than red. I never saw her in anything but her uniform, even when we had a small cocktail party for some dignitaries a year after we began the clinic. She was a full-figured woman with hips a bit too large and hands that were somewhat puffy. Because of her thick shoulders, Ralston joked that she was a man in drag, despite her abundant bosom.

"Thank you. I'll confer with Dr. Price tomorrow," I told her.

"As you wish," she said. She glanced back toward Grace's room and then narrowed her eyes a bit when she turned to say good night to me.

I could feel her staring after me, and as ashamed as I am to admit it, Willow, I walked faster. Imagine, the head doctor being terrorized by his nurse. You'll understand a bit more after you read more.

Miles was waiting for me outside. Alberta was right about his history with me, of course. He had been a patient of mine, thrown into a serious depression after he had caused a car accident that had resulted in the death of his daughter. He had been drunk and was unable to forgive himself. I never told Alberta the full extent of his problems, how many times and in how many different ways he had attempted suicide, but I was confident that he was well enough to take on responsibilities, and he and I had developed an unspoken, almost brotherly trust.

"You all right, Dr. De Beers?" he asked after I had gotten into the car and we had started away from the clinic.

"Yes, fine, Miles."

This was the first time I had asked him to drive me back to the clinic this late in the evening. He was a man of few words now, but he didn't require much conversation to communicate. He watched over me far better than I watched over myself and knew my moods, my emotional status, better than anyone. Certainly, he knew me better than Alberta.

"I heard you lecturing that young Dr. Wheeler the other day," he said. For Miles, that was truly a mouthful.

"Oh?"

"That business about getting so involved with your patient's problems, how you could take them onto yourself almost like a contagious disease."

I laughed. "You were listening carefully, Miles. I am impressed."

"You're not guilty of doing what you warned him about doing, now are you, Dr. De Beers?"

"No, Miles."

"I hope not, Doctor. I don't know enough yet to be your therapist," he added and I laughed.

We both laughed.

It felt wonderful. Willow, it was as if the world was in the process of changing completely for me, shadows moving off of beautiful places, colorful places. I noticed the stars. I took pleasure in the ride home, the road, the foliage, and the trees. I suddenly became aware of my surroundings, and not just the grounds of the clinic or the grounds of our home. For too long those two places had been my entire world. Now the whole world was my world.

And all because I had come face to face with the truth of my heart, Willow.

I was in love, as deeply and terribly in love as anyone ever was.

Impatience set in. I couldn't stand the idea of having to spend the whole night away from Grace. Sleep was an annoyance. I tossed and turned and must have looked at the clock a dozen times, each time disappointed in how slowly time passed. *You're mad,* I told myself repeatedly. *It will come to no good,* I warned myself, but it was that abandon, that great risk that made it all even more exciting, Willow, and up until that moment there wasn't any excitement in my life that could possibly compare.

Courting Alberta and marrying her had been so safe, just another step in my progress toward being the most respected, successful psychiatrist in our state and then the country. I truly was as she accused, following steps in a textbook. As a result I had all the trappings of a successful professional man. The wonderful and impressive home, the fame, and the seemingly perfect wife. I had everything I should have, except I didn't have love.

Before Grace, I didn't think it mattered. I didn't even think it truly existed!

I have to pause. Writing all this has taken away my breath for the moment. I am positive that when you read this, you will think another man wrote it. These are not the words and deeds of the father you have known. Are we all schizophrenics? I'm laughing so hard at that possibility that tears are coming.

What I can assure you of now, what I hope you feel in my words, is the fact that you were born out of love, not lust. You were born to be living proof of what Grace and I had together. No, Willow, you will never, ever be thought of as a mistake in my mind or your mother's. Anything resulting from pure and sincere love has to be good.

A few kisses, holding each other, whispering secrets to each other are not enough to justify those words: *I am in love.* I knew that, but I was worried that Grace did not. She was, after all, still in some mental anguish and turmoil. All I might have done that night was confuse her further.

What began then was a careful, at times meticulously careful, construction of a secret relationship in a place where secrets were meant to be uncovered and purged. Everything we psychiatrists did at the clinic was designed to get our patients to reveal themselves, either through art or dance or words themselves. Together, with their therapists, they had to open those closets and cabinets, put on lights to wash away the darkest places, and confess aloud the deepest, most hidden actions, even things they did not consciously remember. Every layer of their very being had to be stripped away until they stood naked and trusting and began to rebuild themselves.

What had I done, after all, but add another layer of words and actions that must never be exposed? In other words, Willow, the doctor in me was in a rage. If I seemed in any way distracted before, and of course Alberta considered me mentally and emotionally away for quite a while now, I certainly must have appeared more so. Troubled by my actions and confessions, I walked about like a zombie, barely noticing where I was going. Only Miles noticed anything and continually asked me how I was or if there was something else he could do for me.

One day he actually came out and asked, "Are you

having money troubles, Dr. De Beers, because if you are, you can hold off paying me for a while. I'm fine."

"No, of course not, Miles, but thank you for the offer," I told him. Nothing I told him could be more true.

The clinic, being private, was always profitable, but beside that, my sister Agnes and I had inherited a considerable fortune. There was never a time in my life when money was a concern. I had a good business manager, lawyer, and accountant. If anything, I was oblivious to my finances and probably will be to the day I die. My father was far more of a businessman than I am. He knew where his money was to the penny and always had a concept of what things should cost him. If our electric bill or gas bill went over his estimate, he invoked economies, complaining about lights being on unnecessarily or areas of the house having thermostats set too high. He tried to teach me to be a good economist, but I was a poor student, and eventually he gave up and declared I was lucky I was becoming a doctor.

"You'll look after the health of people, and healthy people will look after you," he told me. How wise he was.

I guess what I am telling you is I have been and always will be a man of some contradiction. I spend my working life in the abstract world, searching and analyzing feelings, emotions, dreams, and subconscious thoughts. The physical and material world is mundane to me. Alberta has always complained about my lack of interest in my wardrobe, criticizing me for not keeping in style or wearing shoes and suits until they look ready to be given to charity. She would be the one to stop, look at me, and say, "Time to get a haircut, Claude, and if you are going to wear a beard, you could at least take care to have it trimmed neatly. I'll be too embarrassed to be seen with you, not that I am very much these days," she would mutter.

Her conversation with me became almost rote, a memorized list of comments and sarcasms that I could always anticipate. However, if she didn't point out these things about myself to me, I probably would have gone on and on neglecting them. Suddenly a real change came over me, and it never occurred to me that she would take any notice. That caught me by surprise.

Grace was the first patient with whom I had developed so strong an emotional tie, of course. I wanted to look good for her. Consequently, without Alberta's prodding, I looked after my own appearance, had my hair styled, my beard finely trimmed, and bought some rather attractive new suits, new shoes, and new shirts and belts. I spent more money on my wardrobe that particular week than I had during the last few years.

"Well, well," Alberta said one afternoon when she saw me come home. "When did you buy that suit?"

"Oh," I said, stumbling for an answer. "Ralston had bought something similar and I thought—."

"You thought you were a slob and you should clean up your act, but not for me. Oh, no, for your precious clinic and your nutcases instead."

"If I've told you once, I've told you a million times, Alberta, do not refer to my patients that way, even in jest. Someone will hear you say it, and if the wife of the head doctor says such things—"

"I know, I know, I know. Do you think I even mention the clinic when I'm with people? Whenever anyone brings it up, I tell them I know very little about your work. You're so brilliant. What could a poor, normal person like myself understand? It's not exactly like owning a fine hotel, I tell them, and they appreciate my position. So don't get yourself all worked up and concerned, Claude. I won't embarrass you. All I ask is you give me the same consideration."

"All right, Alberta," I relented. "Thank you."

"And you got yourself a haircut, too. I must say, Claude, you can be a handsome man when you make a little effort."

She smiled and I thought how strange and ironic. *My wife is attracted to me because I'm making myself more attractive to another woman, the woman I love.* Suddenly Alberta was in her own Southern style more flirtatious. Consequently, my guilt made me want to please her more than ever, and I even forced myself to attend two charity events in a row with her.

Whenever I am at any of these occasions, the people who know what I do for a living ask me the most inane questions about my work and my patients. I find I also make people nervous, especially at dinner parties. Alberta has told me that I intimidate some of her friends. They are afraid to speak because they think I will analyze them and find something wrong.

"What do you want me to do?" I asked her.

"Stop being so serious. Tell jokes and never, never look at anyone too intensely," she prescribed. I was never good at telling jokes, but I actually practiced some just to please her.

Willow, I think anyone else would have realized her husband was acting strangely and would have become suspicious. Alberta never did, not even afterward when I had to convince her to take you into our lives.

But I am leaping ahead again. I'm writing this so fast at times, my wrist aches. It's as if I'm afraid I will die before it's completed and you will get only half the story and never know the things I want you to know.

For a while after the night I confessed my love to Grace, we tiptoed around each other. Very conscious of the possibility that Alberta would see something telling in my actions after I declared my love for Grace, I was even more sensitive to the possibility my associates, Ralston especially, would see something very unusual in my relationship with her. Consequently, I know I leaned too far in the opposite direction, which in itself is revealing behavior to a good analyst.

Whenever I spoke to Grace in front of others, my voice was sharp, hard, and almost impatient. I tried to be as formal as I could. I avoided her in the cafeteria and barely acknowledged her in the corridors or in the recreational room. I wrote lengthy reports about our sessions and had Ralston review them, and, for a short period, I did not take her for any walks.

To her credit, Grace understood and never complained. It was enough for us to occasionally exchange a warm, knowing look with each other outside my office. She also appreciated the fact that when she was in my office and we were having a therapeutic session, we should do everything in our power to keep it professional. For a while we were able to do that, and perhaps because Grace trusted me even more now, she was more and more forthcoming.

At a session nearly two weeks later, she confessed her nagging guilt for what had happened between her and Kirby Scott, her mother's third husband, a man I hope you never encounter. I must admit that when she spoke about him in these sessions, I felt terrible pangs of jealousy, Willow.

"Kirby was and I'm sure still is a very handsome, charming man," she told me. "I couldn't help but fantasize about him. He spent a great deal of time with me, always claiming he was doing his best to get me to become more social, more assured of myself when I was with men. My mother even thought it was nice of him to take such an interest in me. Can you imagine?"

"I guess he was a great con man."

"More than just a con man. The devil himself," she said. She shook her head softly. "He would make it all seem instructional," she told me, a faint smile on her lips.

Was it a smile of irony or a smile of real appreciation and excitement? I wondered.

"Why do you smile after saying that?" I asked her, my heart beating with anticipation. There were so many questions I wanted to ask.

And yet how delicate I had to be with her, Willow. How careful about my intonation, my choice of words, my expressions, for how could I do her any good as a therapist if I came at her like some jealous new lover?

"I smile because I can't help thinking how charming and beguiling he was, Claude. He had a way of sneaking up on me, taking me completely by surprise."

"Explain that," I asked, pulling myself together and turning the page of my notebook.

"Before he did something, said something, he would tell me this was how he won the love of a woman, and he would ask me for my reactions as if he were testing himself to see if he was still good at what he did. He made me feel as if I was part of some love practicing so that I wouldn't think of him touching me as me, especially. Do you know what I mean?"

"I think so," I said.

"Then he would take on this very serious expression like a Don Juan instructor or something. 'You can be shy, Grace,' he would say. 'Men like a woman to have some shyness, but you don't want to appear incapable or so innocent they will feel they are taking advantage of you,' which, of course, was exactly what he was doing. 'Flirt, if you like, but at the end of every promise, Grace,' he would say, 'there has to be some delivery. You don't want men to think of you as a tease. Reward the man you love with the warmest part of yourself.'

"He would kiss me and then he would pull back

and look as if he was deciding if I had done it right. I would hold my breath for his judgment, and then he would smile and nod and say something like, 'You are getting the idea.'

"He made me feel like I was becoming a woman, a woman in every sense of his definition, a woman like the sort of woman he would marry."

"You were becoming like your mother, then, mature, beautiful, capable?"

"Yes," she said. "Exactly. I so wanted to be like her. She was independent, strong, and despite all the terrible things that had befallen us, she was able to compete and go on and continue to be strong for the both of us."

"I see," I said.

"Do you, Claude?" Her eyes were filling with tears. "Because I can't stop thinking about it."

"You can't blame yourself for what happened because of that, Grace. He had no business coming into your bedroom and doing what he did."

We stared at each other, pages and pages of thoughts falling around us.

"Maybe . . . maybe I'm no better than he was," I muttered.

She shook her head. "If this is wrong," she said, sniffing back her tears and pulling up her shoulders, "I hope I'm never right."

Willow, when people in love say they feel as if they are moving on a cloud, I understand.

I didn't remember getting up and going to her. I was just there and we were kissing each other and holding each other as if the whole world outside and around us had gone away, left us alone to be who we truly were inside ourselves.

"Tonight," I whispered, my lips grazing her cheek. "Tonight I will come to you."

# 7

# My Buoyancy and Joy

There is definitely something about falling in love that turns you into a little boy or a little girl again, Willow. Just like a child impatient with time that drags itself along like an old person indifferent to your anticipation, I looked at the clock constantly, trying to will the hour and minute hands to move faster. My stomach felt as if small springs were popping and bouncing inside it. I went to the mirror in my bedroom and checked myself a half dozen times. The only difference between me and an anxious teenager was the constant realization that what I was about to do was consummate a love affair, take action that would impact on my life and Grace's forever and ever. It should have given me pause, Willow. It should have stopped me at the door. But as they say, a team of wild horses pulling in the opposite direction couldn't have done so.

I was almost unable to go. Alberta appeared at my bedroom door. I had showered and shaved and dressed in something I thought made me more attractive, a nice light-blue silk shirt I had worn but once. I was actually toying with my hair, experimenting with different ways of brushing it, when she was just there. She was in a nightgown.

"What are you doing?" she asked me.

"Oh, nothing."

"Why are you so nicely dressed?"

"Am I? I thought I hadn't worn this shirt since I bought it and—"

"Oh, forget about it," she said, not really interested in any explanation I might give anyway. "I have a terrible headache and nothing is helping tonight. I want one of those pills you give your patients."

I knew she meant Valium.

"I'm not fond of giving those out like aspirins, Alberta."

"Oh, stop being the doctor for one moment and be my husband. I had too much champagne this afternoon. That's all and I need something to help me relax. I'm on pins and needles. The election for president of the Woman's Club is being held tomorrow, and you know I'm running against two other women, neither of whom deserve it nor have worked as hard as I have for the organization."

I stared at her.

"You do remember the election, don't you, Claude? You do remember I was running for president?"

"Oh, yes. I just forgot how soon it was."

"How could you do that?"

"I'm sorry."

"You should have that expression tattooed on your forehead, Claude. *I'm sorry. I'm sorry.* Look, I need to relax," she insisted.

"Okay, okay." I thought a moment and then found some Valium for her. It was a weak dosage, but enough to do what she wanted done. Nevertheless, I felt evil, Willow. I felt as if I was putting her in a fog just so she wouldn't know what I was about to do and would do.

I gave her the pills and she returned to her own room to sleep and face the results of her Woman's Club election the following day. If she lost, which was in my mind very likely, she would be very difficult.

Since I hadn't told Miles anything about my plans, I expected he would be retired for the evening, but he surprised me and appeared the moment I came downstairs and headed toward the front entrance.

"Did I forget something on the schedule, Doctor?" he asked.

"Oh, no, Miles. It's something that just came up. It's all right. I'll drive myself back to the clinic."

"It's no problem for me, Doctor. I have no pressing engagements," he added.

I was caught in so many deceits and webs of my own making, Willow. Now I was even lying to Miles. If I refused his offer, he would be upset. I could see it in his face. He needed to be needed, and yet, having him drive me made me feel I was making him part of what I was doing, and I thought that was wrong.

Feeling cornered, I smiled and nodded and told him to get the car.

I glanced at the stairway, looking up toward Alberta's bedroom and thinking she was falling asleep with never a thought of what I was about to do ever crossing her mind. A part of me wanted to have me march back up those stairs and throw open her door to declare, "Alberta, I am in love with another woman. I cannot continue this pretense."

And yet there was another part of me that still couldn't believe I would do what I was setting out to do. Even when I was sitting in the vehicle and we were driving to the clinic, I heard this voice within me taunting, *You can't do this, Claude De Beers. You are only fooling yourself. You will embarrass yourself. You will fall on your face and in front of the whole staff and even some patients. Tell Miles to turn back. Turn back before it's too late.*

If those words were there, my tongue refused to form them. I closed my eyes and thought only of Grace, Grace waiting for me in her room, Grace trembling with expectation and with hope, keeping the demons outside her door, staring away any shadows, closing her own ears to any warnings.

Of course, I wondered if she loved me out of a terrible need born from her mental problems or if she loved me as purely and as overwhelmingly as I loved her. Shouldn't I be able to tell? *You're an analyst, analyze,* I told myself. In my heart I knew I was too much in love, too compromised even to attempt such an objective evaluation.

More to the point, did I want even to consider the question? I wanted her and that overwhelmed everything else, even her own state of mind. Was I horrible, Willow? Was I terrible to think such thoughts?

*Drive on, Miles,* I thought. *Take me to my love, to my destiny and all else be damned.*

Maybe it was because of the excitement boiling inside me, or maybe it was more what I wished than what was, but when I looked up at the night sky, it seemed to be particularly full of stars, so crowded with the twinkling specks they looked as if they might bump into each other. The Big Dipper was never clearer. I vowed that I would forget nothing about this night. I would memorize the heavens so that afterward, every time I thought about this evening, I would see that sky and I would feel the same electric excitation and joy.

"I'll be in the recreation room," Miles told me after we parked and I started for the front entrance of the clinic.

"What? Oh, yes," I said. "Good."

Can you believe it, Willow? I actually forgot he was there, walking just behind me. My mind was so focused on Grace. Self-conscious now, I slowed down, pulled myself back, and tried to look more like the doctor than an anxious lover.

Nadine Gordon was not on duty that evening, thankfully. Suzanne Cohen, a much gentler nurse, younger, but just as competent, was in the recreation room speaking softly to a new patient of ours, whom I will call Palmer. He was a twelve-year-old boy who had been acting out more and more seriously, finally setting fire to his own home. Ralston had taken the lead therapist position with him. He was, I will admit, better with teenagers than I was. In any case Suzanne did not notice my entrance, but would of course realize I was there as soon as Miles appeared.

I went to my office and busied myself with some reports, anticipating Suzanne coming around to see if there was anything in particular I needed from her. Less then ten minutes later she appeared.

"Everything is fine," I told her. "Please, just go about your usual duties, Suzanne."

"I thought I should tell you that Grace Montgomery retired early tonight," she said. "I thought she looked more distracted than she has these past few weeks. She didn't eat very well at dinner, either."

"Oh? Well, I'll try to stop by to see her. Thanks, Suzanne."

She stood there for a moment longer. My heart was ticking away like a time bomb. Had Grace done something, said something about us?

"Very good, Doctor. I'll be at my station should you need me for anything."

"Thank you," I said, still holding my breath until she actually left my office.

I closed the files and sat back. The reasonable doctor part of me began its final pleas, its final attempt at turning me back.

*Just put everything away here, Claude. Find Miles and go home,* I heard the voice inside me advise. *Before it's too late, forever too late, go home, Claude. Go home.*

When I stood up and walked to my office door, I actually did not know which way I would go, Willow. I thought of that famous poem by Robert Frost. You know, the one about someone stopping at a fork in the road and choosing one direction over the other and Frost concluding it made all the difference. How many forks in the road do we come to in our lives? I wondered. How many choices do we make that truly affect everything else ahead of us?

And that made all the difference, I kept thinking as I walked toward the patient dormitory and Grace's room, where I knew she waited for me.

She had the small lamp lit on her nightstand, and she was in bed, reading. She looked up when I entered, but she said nothing. I stood there gazing at her. What was the magic that held me so firmly, orbiting her every gesture, every smile, longing to touch her hair, kiss her lips, hold her close to my heart? Was it all some chemical, physical thing or is there truly such a thing as soul mates? I wondered and still do. I laughed to myself thinking how surprised my colleagues would be if I ever so much as brought up such a question for discussion at one of our seminars.

I moved slowly to the side of her bed, neither of us saying a word yet. I think we were both hoping to keep the entire encounter dreamlike, ethereal, perhaps so we could live with it afterward, pretend it was still part of a fantasy.

She closed her book slowly and laid it on the nightstand. I went to my knees and lowered my head gently against her breasts, and she touched my hair. Finally I found some words.

"I wanted to be here so much, to come to you so much, I ache," I said.

With her hands beneath my chin, she lifted my head so we could look into each other's eyes, and then she urged me toward her so our lips would touch, just graze at first and then make demands on each other. That kiss was long and wonderful. I felt myself gliding down some very soft slope. She shifted over in her bed, and I prepared myself to be beside her.

We were like two teenagers first discovering the wonder of our bodies and the power that came from each touch, each kiss. Every moment was new, the unwrapping of another amazing gift of life and of love. We were both so absorbed in each other's warmth and desire, neither of us thought about tomorrow. There were no consequences. There was no price to pay, no repentance to be sought. Nothing mattered more than the moment.

"I have never made love like this," I whispered.

"How can that be?" she wanted to know. "You're married."

"With my wife it's mechanical. It's a performance. Neither of us has ever been ourselves. I have no words to explain this, Grace, no textbook to turn to so that I can find a description of my feelings for you. I am like an atheist who has found there is a God, there is something more than what we can touch and see, hear and taste."

She turned into me and we held each other and

made love to each other and found ourselves deeper and deeper within each other's very being. I was with her for hours, losing all sense of time or place. Finally she fell asleep in my arms, and I released her gently and got dressed. I can't tell you how painful it was to leave her bedside that night, Willow. Twice I turned back to touch her, to kiss her. Her eyelids barely twitched. She had fallen asleep with this most wonderful, yes, angelic smile on her lips. She never looked more content, more secure and happy with herself than she did at that moment. It made me feel as if I had truly done a wonderful thing, not only for myself, but for her and for whatever we were together.

The act of love does create a new entity, Willow, if it is with someone you truly do love. You become so merged, so much a part of each other that there is a birth. I and you become we, and that, I thought then, and I think still, is a real miracle and not one that any textbook can explain.

Finally, like one tearing free of powerful chains, I managed to get the strength to leave her. I stepped into the quiet, brightly lit hallway, the harshness of the illumination shocking me back to my reality. I glanced at my watch and was astounded at how long I had been with Grace.

I hurried down to the recreation room and found Miles asleep on the sofa, the television blinking like a hypnotist's light, throwing shadows on the walls. For a moment I was at a loss about what to do. Wake him, of course, but how did I explain this late hour? Where was the night staff? I nudged him and he opened his eyes, gazed at me in confusion for a moment, and then sat up quickly.

"Oh, Doctor, sorry," he said, grinding the sleep out of his eyes.

"Let's go home, Miles," I said quickly.

"What time is it?" he asked and looked at his watch. "Well, I'll be darned," he muttered.

I was already out in the hallway. I was in flight, hoping none of the staff would see me and wonder why I was still there. Miles trailed behind, muttering to himself. I could hear the low murmur of conversation coming from the cafeteria. When we passed the doorway, I did not look in and hoped no one was looking out. Moments later I was in my automobile.

Miles got in quickly and started the engine.

"This was a late one for you, Dr. De Beers," he commented.

"To be honest, Miles," I said, "I dozed off myself."

"Oh," he said and nodded. "No problem. But I've been telling you that you're working too hard," he chastised.

"You might be right," I said.

My house was as quiet as the clinic had been. Alberta was long asleep, I thought as I made my way up the stairs. The Valium surely relaxed her enough. She rarely checked to see if I was in my bedroom anyway. If something else disturbed her and she went looking for me in my office and saw I was not there, I was sure she gave up thinking about my whereabouts and attended to herself. Even so, I was extra quiet when I reached her bedroom door.

I went to bed as quickly as I could, but I could not fall asleep for the life of me, Willow. Instead, I lay there thinking about Grace, still smelling the aroma of her hair and reliving the taste of her lips and the softness of her body. I replayed every word we had uttered to each other. Finally I curled around my pillow and hugged it like a lovesick teenager, which enabled me to drift into some repose.

I overslept and rose quite late. In fact, I rose so late, Alberta was up before me. What a panic it put me in. Miles was more troubled by it than I was. He came to my room as I was dressing.

"Oh, good, you're up finally. I went to your door twice, Doctor," he said, "and knocked pretty hard, I must say. I thought you might have been in the bathroom, but I did look in on you and saw you were dead to the world. Who was I to wake you?" he asked.

"It's all right, Miles."

"Dr. Ralston called," he told me. Then he leaned toward me and whispered, "Mrs. De Beers spoke to him, not me."

"Oh?"

"I know he asked her if she knew why you had returned to the clinic because I heard her say, 'I didn't know he had returned. I'm surprised he bothers coming home.' "

"It's okay, Miles," I said. By reporting what he had overheard, he was, without realizing it, making me feel worse, making me feel as if he and I were conspirators, plotters in some way.

He nodded and left me.

"What's wrong with you? Are you sick?" Alberta asked when I appeared downstairs. She was having her morning coffee and nibbling like a squirrel on her toast. I could see she was quite agitated. She hadn't taken as perfect care of her coiffure. It was unlike her to have a single strand out of place. Her eyes were electric with anxiety. It wasn't because of me, however. It was because of her Woman's Club election.

"No, just a little tired," I said.

"How can you be so tired? What do you do over there but sit and talk to mentally disturbed people? I wouldn't even call it talking. Question after question. 'Why do you hate your mother? Why do you hate your father?' If they aren't crazy when they arrive, they are before they leave," she muttered.

Whenever something bothered her, no matter how small or big it was, she relieved herself by being critical of me and my profession. Usually, if I paid little attention to it and barely defended myself, she would soon stop.

"Someone asked me the other day," she continued, whipping her words at me. "I think it was Sara Marshall. Yes, it was Sara Marshall. She asked me if you do those horrible shock things to people, and I told her I had no idea what you do over there. Do you?"

"No, Alberta. We don't."

"That's a relief," she said. She looked at the clock and sighed deeply. "The counting has begun," she said.

"Oh?"

"I'm not going to sit around here all day like some woman in labor and wait for the phone call. They'll have to find me."

"I wish you luck, Alberta," I said. She looked up at me and stared for a long moment, just like someone trying desperately to remember something.

"Oh, yes," she said. "That Dr. Price called asking after you. He said you were at the clinic last night. I told him he was mistaken. You were home. Weren't you home, Claude?"

I looked away to avoid her. Willow, I felt like a little boy caught with his hand in the cookie jar, but when I looked back at her, I realized Alberta's eyes were too clouded with her own concerns to see anything in my face.

"I had to check on something, yes," I said.

"You ought to just move in there, Claude. Turn one of the looney bin rooms into a second bedroom for yourself," she said. She put her coffee cup down so sharply, it almost shattered. "I'm not sitting around here waiting for them to call," she repeated, stood up, and started out of the dining room. At the door she paused. "If I have any good news to tell you later, I'll call the clinic. I have no doubt you'll be there," she added and left.

The whole time she had been with me, I had been intermittently holding my breath. The air was so still and stagnant in the room, I felt as if I was shut up in a house without windows. Tiny beads of sweat had formed on my forehead, in fact. I wiped my face with my napkin and then rose to go to the clinic. Miles was waiting for me outside, speaking to one of the grounds people. He looked up as soon as I appeared.

"You all right, Doctor?"

"Fine, Miles. Let's go," I said and he moved quickly.

What a mess I felt I was in now, Willow. I was worried about explaining myself to Ralston, of course, but as we drove to the clinic, I was also very much concerned and worried about Grace. What would be the effect on her of what we had done the night before? Was Ralston looking for me because of her behavior today? Had I caused some terrible regression or exacerbated her problems? Her mother, your grandmother, had brought her to me to help her, to make her well enough to return to their world. Had my selfish acts made that all be impossible now?

Saying I was tense doesn't do justice to how I felt when I entered the clinic. Ralston was in a session with Palmer, so I had some breathing room there. Nadine Gordon was attending to some other patients, but she was the first to inquire as to my health.

"I'm fine," I told her.

"You do work too hard, Doctor," she said, surprising me with the softness in her voice. "I might not show it, but I worry about you."

"Thank you for your concern, Ms. Gordon. I'm all right."

"You try too hard with some of our patients, Doctor. No one should expect miracles of you."

I nodded.

"Any particular problems this morning?" I asked.

She stared at me a long moment. Did she know that I was really inquiring only about Grace?

"No," she said. "Your Miss Montgomery . . ."

"Yes?" I said, trying not to appear overly interested.

"Is very chipper and energetic today. In fact, she's in the arts and crafts room helping Miss Richards with the other patients. One would think she was one of our attendants. She practically begged me not to make her take her medication this morning, claiming she had no need of it.

"I told her when she graduated medical school, I would take orders from her," she added dryly.

"Interesting," I said.

"Yes, isn't it?" she pursued, her eyes a bit smaller. "Maybe it will give you the opportunity to spend more time with your other patients now," she suggested with a cold, calculating smile that went right to my heart.

"Maybe," I said, nodding. "I'll look into it."

She held her eyes on me and then she turned and left the office.

Later, when Grace appeared for her session with me, I saw Nadine Gordon in the hallway. She didn't look away when I looked at her. Grace walked in and I stood there in the doorway exchanging this inquisitive glance with my head nurse. She gave me a small nod and left. I closed the door and turned to Grace.

"How are you?" I asked her.

She answered by rising on the balls of her feet to kiss me softly on the lips.

And then she smiled and said, "I wanted to be sure it wasn't all a dream."

"Are you sure?"

"Yes," she said.

"How?"

"From the look on your face," she replied, and I laughed and reached out to embrace her.

We held on to each other like two castaways who had found a welcoming shore and knew we would never be alone again.

Later that day my receptionist Edith Hamilton buzzed me in my office to tell me Alberta absolutely insisted I pick up the phone. It mattered not whether I was in a session with a patient or not. I could tell Alberta had flustered Edith because she kept apologizing for interrupting me. I told Edith it was fine and had her pass Alberta's call through.

"What's wrong?" I asked immediately.

"Wrong? Why don't you ask what's right for a change? Must all you psychiatrists always look to the dark side of things?"

"I'm sorry, Alberta. My receptionist said—"

"That woman was rude to me. When I call your precious clinic, they should be told it's important and I'm not to hear any 'Can I have him call you back?' Or 'He's with a patient.' "

"Sometimes it is very important not to be interrupted, Alberta," I said calmly. "Okay. Why are you calling with such urgency?"

"It's not urgency, Claude. It's elation, something you're not accustomed to seeing over there in your inner sanctum and halls of misery."

"Elation?"

"I was elected," she declared. "You're speaking to the new president of the Woman's Club."

"Oh. Congratulations, Alberta. That's very nice," I said.

"Nice? Nice? Why is it you always have the perfect words for your mentally disturbed patients and their families, but not for me? *Nice?* It's more than just nice, Claude."

"I didn't mean it was just nice, Alberta. I meant it was nice that they appreciate you and your great efforts to make the organization a success," I said.

She was satisfied with that.

"Well?" she added.

"Well, what?"

"How do you intend to celebrate this with me?"

"Oh. Well, why don't we go to the Hideaway?" I said. It was the restaurant we had gone to on three previous wedding anniversaries.

"Yes, that would be appropriate," she replied. "I'm surprised you came up with it. Very good, Claude. You might make the husband of a president yet," she added with a light laugh attached. "Go back to your depressing activities and save all your buoyancy and joy for me," she commanded.

If she only knew, I thought, where I had invested all my so-called buoyancy and joy.

# 8

# Wings of Wax

Perhaps nothing fills your heart with optimism and blinds you to reality as much as falling in love does, Willow. When your mother and I were togther, none of the problems I had to face outside the clinic seemed to matter to me. I've already told you that it wasn't that long after our marriage that Alberta began accusing me of indifference toward things that mattered very much to her. I didn't agonize at all over the decisions she made for our home, and I never gave much importance to the social problems she had. In her eyes it wasn't possible for me to be any more neglectful or unconcerned than I already was, so I understand why she didn't take any more notice of my indifference toward anything but the clinic and Grace.

For a while then, I lived in almost as much illusion

as some of my patients. To think that now that I had found Grace I would never feel alone again was foolish, especially for a man who had the education and experience I had. Oh, the self-analysis I ended up doing, Willow, the hours and hours I spent reviewing it all, questioning my own thoughts and feelings. It was truly enough to drive anyone mad. I'm surprised I didn't walk into walls. I was that distracted at times, especially at home, where I paced and spent my time trying to come up with more reasons and more ways to spend even more time at the clinic without attracting too much attention.

To my own credit, I will say that I never once denied the fact that this was a forbidden love affair, Willow. Of course, I tried to conceive of ways to make that not so, but in the end I realized that no one would see it as anything else but a serious violation of my medical ethics. My career, my value to other patients, my whole purpose for being was in great jeopardy, and I had put it there.

Every time your grandmother called that fact was driven home, and the two times she visited the clinic to see Grace made it even more emphatic. The first time was only a little more than a month after Grace and I had become lovers. As strange as it may sound to you, Willow, the worst fear I had was not that somehow Jackie Lee Montgomery would come to realize something was going on between your mother and me. No, the worst fear I had was she would see the changes in your mother that were improvements and insist she be released. Don't forget it was embarrassing to her that your mother was here in the first place.

From the tone and context of phone conversations I had with Jackie Lee, I could also tell that she was becoming unhappy with the ruse of her being Linden's mother. He was getting older and more demanding. Raising a child again was a big responsibility and, without any help, a great burden on her time and her energy. From what she was telling me, I understood that she wanted the freedom to become an eligible widow again, a woman without any baggage so she could sink her teeth into a new husband, preferably someone with good standing in the Palm Beach community and of course, someone wealthy enough to return her to her previous lifestyle. She had lost so much with Kyle Scott: the plane, the boat, the big house, the seemingly unlimited allowance for designer clothing, vacation expenses, everything that was once very important to her and had become so again. Her complaints about her present life seemed to multiply as fast as rabbits and become an endless tail to her inquiries about Grace.

"That man," she would say, "didn't only damage my daughter. He ruined my life and made it so much more difficult. You have to be seen in fine places to meet fine people, especially decent men."

On and on she would go, perhaps thinking I would somehow provide a solution or, at minimum, be sympathetic.

And then, as I said, she began to complain more specifically about her motherhood responsibilities and the toll that was taking on her physically and mentally.

"My daughter should realize she has an obligation to the child," she told me. "Can't you get that through to her, drum that into her head?"

"We don't exactly force these things on our patients, Jackie Lee. Your daughter has to arrive at the conclusions by herself or they won't be lasting, and that's what we both want, isn't it?"

I wanted to ask her whatever happened to her worry that Grace wouldn't be able to handle motherhood, her concern that once someone had a mental problem, it was always there, never corrected.

"I've been through all this sort of responsibility already," she wailed. "I need my freedom, too. A grandmother should be a visitor," she told me. "She should be able to shut her doors, say goodbye, drive away. None of the grandmothers I know are anything like I am today. I feel like I'm being punished for my daughter's sins and not vice versa.

"And you were right the first time," she continued, "it's not good for the child. He'll be so terribly confused. He'll end up in your clinic, too!"

I tried my best to commiserate with her, but I couldn't get up enough sincerity to make myself sound convincing, especially to myself. First, I didn't appreciate Jackie Lee's real motives for wanting Grace to be released, and second, I dreaded the day she would leave the clinic.

In any case Jackie Lee arrived at the clinic, or more like charged at it. For someone complaining about how hard and stressful her life had become, she looked absolutely glamorous. As stylish and elegant as the first time I had met her, she entered my office with great expectation. Grace and she had spoken a number of times on the telephone, and from the last two conversations she had with her, Jackie Lee was convinced that Grace was as close to being normal as she could ever be.

"She asked about Linden. She sounded very homesick, and she didn't mention any ghosts or her father or Kyle. You've done a wonderful job," she declared with a definite sense of finality. I had the sense she would jump up at any moment and start packing Grace's bags.

"Thank you, Jackie Lee, but I'm afraid we'd be moving things a little too quickly if we sent her home right now."

"Why? What else is there to do?" she wailed, her face filled with disappointment and frustration.

"She's still dependent on medication and—"

"Oh, if that's all, I can certainly give her pills, make sure she takes them on time and everything."

"No, it's not just the dispensing of the medicines, it's the monitoring and regulation of them that's important, and there are still a number of troubling issues to work out through therapy. Remember I asked you to be patient. Now, you wouldn't want to cause a relapse here. It's often more difficult to return to this stage of improvement once something like that occurs," I warned her. "It could be worse, in fact."

Part of it was true, but part of it was my selfish conniving to keep her from taking Grace away from me.

She lowered her shoulders like a flag of defeat.

"This is so hard, so hard," she muttered.

"I know," I said. "I appreciate what you are going through. Believe me, we want only the best for the both of you, for all of you."

"Well, let's see how she is," she told me, and I brought her to visit with Grace, who was sitting on a bench in the garden and reading.

Grace knew her mother was coming, of course. She and I had discussed it. I had not dared tell her my fears, but she knew from speaking with her mother that Jackie Lee anticipated taking her home, if not now, very soon. When Grace told me about the conversations, I said nothing more than a "We'll see." I was afraid of what I would say if I added any more. Apparently, she understood.

"You look wonderful," Jackie Lee declared the moment Grace lifted her eyes from the pages of the book she was reading. "What a difference between the girl I brought here and the girl I'm now looking at, wouldn't you agree, Dr. De Beers?" she asked.

Grace and I looked at each other.

"There's been some marked improvement, yes," I said, stressing the word *some*.

"Um," Jackie Lee grunted.

"I'll leave you two for a while," I said, backing away. "I have to attend to some matters."

"Go on, Doctor. Thank you," Jackie Lee said, smiling at Grace. "I can see we don't need you hovering over us."

She sat beside Grace, who looked at me with some desperation in her eyes. I nodded, smiled at her, and left them, my heart pounding with anxiety. My feelings were mixed, of course, and I was at myself again, chastising myself for being so selfish as to want to keep a patient longer than she might need to be kept. I made up my mind that I would have Ralston treat her for a while so he could make an evaluation.

I am writing all this as if it is only my story. In the beginning of all this, I did not fully consider Grace's feelings, Willow. She was just as troubled by mixed emotions and desires as I was. On the one hand, I was sure she very much wanted to be considered well enough to go home. She certainly wanted either me or Dr. Price to confirm that she was capable of raising her child.

On the other hand, she was truly in love with me, and she never felt safer than she did with me at the clinic. In our own little world, no demon could enter and spoil anything. The curse she had come to believe was on her and followed her through most of her young life was stopped outside the door. I was too powerful for it. It dared not show its dark face.

"I can love you and not be afraid for you or for myself," she told me once.

There was that contradiction in me again, Willow. The doctor part of me insisted that was not valid. She would be just as safe anywhere and I had no special powers, certainly no powers to overcome some curse, and if there was one thing I didn't want to do as a psychotherapist, it was to provide her with another crutch. However, I would be lying if I didn't confess that the other part of me, the man, the lover, wanted to encourage such thoughts because I knew they would keep her close to me.

What would end such a grand struggle for my and her destinies? Apparently, at the end of that first visit, I knew it wasn't going to be Jackie Lee. Grace either pretended or really believed she was not quite ready to be released and return. She convinced her mother that she was still too fragile. I believed that, too, but I needed to have it validated, and so I told her I was going to have her see Dr. Price for the next few weeks. There was a danger in that, of course. Ralston was a talented man, a very perceptive man. He might very well discover the true relationship between Grace and me, and I wasn't ready for him to know that, nor was she.

The fact is she fell into a bad depression when she began her sessions with him. Not only didn't she make any new progress, she began to regress and to the point where he confronted me.

"Why did you want me to take this patient now, Claude?" he asked me. "You were doing so well with her. Now she's practically the way she was the day she arrived."

I referred to my original intention, talking about Jackie Lee and how she was pressuring me to release Grace. I wanted to be sure I was doing the right thing by resisting. He was too clever to buy into that completely. I could see it in the way he tilted his head and gave me his famous, "Umm."

"Well, I'm afraid I'm not doing well with her, Claude. She has a better rapport with you. I would advise you to continue her therapy. She's built a trust with you, a bridge that I'm only blocking.

"As for the mother, you're handling her correctly," he concluded, and Grace returned to me.

After that I spent more and more time at the clinic, taking advantage of Alberta's new and heavier involvement in her social activities since being elected president of her favorite club. She was out planning fundraisers, socials, networking with other women and other organizations, especially charities. She was almost weekly in the social pages of our newspapers and featured twice on our local television stations.

One afternoon Grace and I took one of our now famous walks, only we didn't stop at the crest nor did we stop at the river's edge. We continued on until we found a beautiful area shaded by trees. I knew we had gone too far from the clinic, and it would take us too long to return, but it was a magnificent, beautiful day with the sort of sky artists envision, the blue deep and rich, the few clouds puffy and milk white.

We sat on a soft patch of grass and watched a flock of birds do amazing gymnastic-like turns and circles. It was as though they were performing for us.

"When we first moved to our estate on the beach," Grace said, "I used to go out at night and lay on the sand and look up at the starry sky. Soon I would feel like I was falling into it, like I was above the stars."

She lay back and put her hands behind her head and looked up at the clouds.

"Try it," she told me, and I lay beside her.

"Yes," I said, laughing. "It works."

We were both very still, hardly breathing for fear of shattering the moment.

"What will become of us, Claude?" she finally asked me.

"You will get stronger and you will return to your boy," I said.

"That's me. What about us, Claude?"

"I don't know," I said. "I know what I wish and want, but I don't know, Grace. It's very complicated with your being my patient and all."

"You're so honest with me," she said, turning and bracing herself on her elbow. "You could easily make up a fantasy, tell me a story, give me some false hope, but you won't."

"I try to give it to myself and fail," I said, smiling.

"What else is there but the moment, the here and now anyway?" she asked, laughing with a wonderfully pure abandon. Then she stopped, held my gaze in hers for a moment before she leaned down and kissed me. I closed my eyes and willed this all to be forever and ever, willed away any obstacles.

We made love in that field that day, Willow, and there is no doubt in my mind, that was the day you were conceived. How many children get to know that, the where and the when and the beauty of the moment? I hope you cherish this revelation and see it for the wonderful time it was. Perhaps now you can understand why I would not trade a moment, not erase a second of my life with your mother.

When we returned and Nadine Gordon practically attacked me with the news I had kept another patient waiting too long for his session, I should have realized that things would become more and more difficult. But my heart was too full. Even her ice-cold eyes and granite-like face of chastisement couldn't shake me. Behind her back, I held Grace's hand in mine and then I let her go and went on to do my work.

Little did I know that day that what would end the grand struggle for Grace's and my destinies had taken place: your conception.

I'm sure you're wondering why I was so careless. Here I was a man of science, a logical, reasonable man who was spending his adult life helping other people avoid mistakes that would impact on their lives, and I, your efficient, meticulous, and dedicated professional father, behaved like nothing more than a foolish teenager. What was I thinking?

If I bother analyzing myself, I might conclude that I wanted this relationship so much, Willow, I was willing at least subconsciously to risk everything to have it. I permitted myself to believe that should Grace become pregnant with my child, we would be together forever. You were to make that happen.

Of course, nothing could be more romantic and foolish on my part. Not only would I destroy my own life and career, I would damage Grace, and who knew what Jackie Lee would do about that? Ironically, by not thinking about birth control, all I had really accomplished was to drive the love of my life from me.

It didn't happen for some time, of course. Over the next few weeks and months, Grace did exactly what she had done before when she was pregnant with Linden. She revealed nothing. But to be fair to her, she was caught in a new turmoil herself and not a new turmoil of her own making. And I am not just speaking of my actions, Willow.

Not long after Jackie Lee's first visit and Grace's and my walk to the river, a dark shadow resembling the dark shadows Sandy hallucinated came into Grace's life, or should I say our lives? It began subtly.

First, I noticed how tired Grace often was. I asked her about this during one of our doctor-patient sessions, and she told me she was having strange dreams lately. They did resemble vivid hallucinations. She woke often during the night, and one night she woke screaming. The nurse on duty that evening, Suzanne Cohen, had a report for me in the morning. Of course, I looked into it immediately.

My first terrible fear, Willow, was that my relationship with Grace and the conflicts it was creating in her were bringing about this new emotional and mental problem. I tried observing her unnoticed, especially when she was in the recreation room or the arts and crafts area, and I saw how frequently she looked distracted, even dazed. When I questioned her more and more about it, she grew more and more fragile, often bursting into tears, crying she didn't know why she wasn't sleeping, she didn't know why she was having terrible nightmares.

I began to wonder if her medications weren't being dispensed correctly and did check into it to find some errors in dosages during Nadine Gordon's shifts. This was very uncharacteristic of her, and she apologized profusely. For a while that seemed to correct things.

And then, a terrible crisis occurred. I arrived at the clinic in the morning and found bedlam and tumult going on in the patients' dormitory. I hurried to it where I discovered Dr. Wheeler trying to calm Grace. Her hysterics had triggered Sandy, who was screaming in the hallway and pounding her fists at the walls to drive away those dark shadows she still saw everywhere. Other patients were agitated as well, and my staff was fully involved, attendants and our two additional nurses working on calming everyone. Ralston came flying in after me.

"What's happening?" I cried, rushing to Grace's door.

Nadine Gordon stepped out and glared at me for a moment before saying, "Someone took her teddy bear."

"What?"

Obviously, because of the nature of our patients, we couldn't put locks on their bedroom doors. We couldn't permit them to have the ability to shut themselves in and away from us. From time to time, one or another patient did wander into the wrong room or take someone else's things.

I charged in and saw Wheeler was about to give Grace some sedation. She had torn her room apart looking for her teddy bear. The lamp on the nightstand was shattered on the floor and lay there along with all the spilled drawers. The bed had been ripped at, and the small desk in the corner was turned upside down.

"What is it?" Ralston asked me.

"Her teddy bear's gone," I said, now very frightened for the both of us. She was looking directly at me and crying. "It was a very special gift from her father.

"Hold off, Dr. Wheeler," I ordered. "I'll see to her," I said. "Help with the others."

He looked at Ralston, who nodded, and then he handed me the syringe and left the room. Nadine Gordon stood in the doorway watching and waiting for further orders. I sat on the bed and took Grace's hand in mine. Her sobs shook her body, but she had her lips clamped shut. There was a slight scratch at the side of her left temple where she either had clawed herself in desperation or grazed her head against something during her frantic search.

"It's all right, Grace," I said. "We'll find it."

Her lips trembled so hard, I thought her face would shatter right before my eyes.

Sandy's screaming turned Ralston away from the scene and made him snap an order at Nurse Gordon. He and she left the room to see about the commotion.

"Daddy . . ." Grace managed. ". . . gave it to me."

"I know. Someone must have just seen it and taken it by mistake. I'll turn the clinic inside out until I find it for you. I promise, Grace."

She looked only slightly relieved. My overwhelming love for her had blinded me to the fact that she was still quite emotionally frail and delicate. I was so angry at myself, Willow. I had so wanted Grace to be strong and healthy for me that I avoided all the signs telling me otherwise. If anything should have brought home my professional neglect and malpractice, this should have been it.

It did and I vowed to myself that I would pull back and spend more time as her doctor and not as her lover. I could see her realizing and perhaps hoping this was so, too. She looked at me with the sort of plea and desperation in her eyes that I had seen in many of my other patients: this cry for help that even they didn't realize they were making.

Of course, I would be dishonest if I didn't tell you that I was afraid she would either do or say something which would reveal our relationship. Ralston was back in the room. I gave her the sedative and urged her to sleep, promising I would find her teddy bear. She said nothing. She turned her head and soon afterward she fell asleep.

"I have noticed a change in her these past few weeks, Claude," Ralston said when we both stepped back. "Maybe you're reducing her medications too quickly," he suggested.

"I'll look into it," I said, not wanting to get too deeply into her situation at that moment.

The hallway was cleared. Sandy was medicated and the other patients were guided back to their activities. Nadine Gordon joined us in the hallway.

"Do you know anything about this teddy bear of hers?" I asked quickly.

"I haven't seen it, but I haven't gone looking for it, either," she said.

"What about Sandy?" Ralston asked. "Have you checked her room?"

"Not yet, but I will," she said. "I have noticed that Grace Montgomery was more agitated these days and that was after her medications had been corrected," she added before I could say anything. "She hasn't done anything in the arts and crafts room. She doesn't have the patience to read or watch television lately, either. I was going to bring it to your attention at our next patients' meeting. I don't believe we are at the proper dosages with her yet," she added.

"Claude?" Ralston asked.

"Yes," I said. "She's right. I'll reconsider her medications and get on it," I said.

"What a shame. The girl was making such progress, I actually thought you would please her mother very soon," Ralston said.

"I did as well," Nadine interjected. She held her eyes on me a moment, and then she added, "I'll search Sandy's room."

We watched her leave.

"Careful, Claude," Ralston advised in a very unspecific way. "Wings of wax," he muttered and left me standing outside Grace's doorway, feeling as if I were truly in the midst of a great descent.

# 9

# The Teddy Bear's Arm

The teddy bear was nowhere to be found, Willow. I literally did turn the clinic inside out, spending every available minute looking for it. I had the kitchen staff search every cabinet and shelf. I ordered the attendants to look under every bed. I had Joan Richards take apart her arts and crafts area, and then I had the custodians search the outside of the clinic, especially under or around every window.

How could such a thing disappear into thin air? It was puzzle enough for me, but to Grace it began to corroborate one of her old fears and revive problems I thought we had resolved. When Jackie Lee heard about Grace's regression, she threatened to take her from the clinic and have her put somewhere else. She phoned me, shouting hysterically at times.

"Why did this happen? She was almost cured,

wasn't she? Maybe I was right. It was time to take her out. Maybe the longer she is around those other disturbed people, the worse it will be for her," she said, practically lunging at me through the phone.

"No, no, Jackie Lee," I said. "If she can have this sort of setback while she is here, it could be worse for her and for you if it happened out there," I reasoned. It gave her some pause.

"Well, what do you expect now? What are you going to do about this?"

"I'm reviewing her treatments. Give me a little time."

"Time! That's all you doctors want, time, and of course, money," she chastised.

I was silent.

"All right," she said, relenting. "But I want a weekly report now. If you can't do it yourself, have your secretary call me or a nurse."

"Very good," I said.

"This teddy bear thing. It's inexcusable."

"I agree. I'm not giving up on finding it for her," I promised.

"Maybe she hid it herself somewhere," she suggested. "Maybe she wants to be crazy."

"I don't think so, Jackie Lee. No one could enjoy that sort of pain."

"In the state of mind she's in, anything's possible," she muttered.

Then she went into a rant about her own state of mind and how difficult things were for her.

"People know the truth, you know. I've done the

best I can to prevent it, but they find these things out eventually. They know where she is and they talk about us. They even know about Linden. People feed on this sort of thing here. Now I don't know what will become of her."

I wanted to say I didn't, either, that perhaps Grace would be here a long time if not forever, but I kept my secret thoughts locked in my heart and did the best I could to relieve her of her anxieties.

Soon afterward Grace began to accept the disappearance of her teddy bear the same way she had learned to accept the death of her father. She went into a period of deep mourning, retreating to the shadows in her room, spending hours and hours staring into space, occasionally permitting a fugitive tear to trickle down her cheek and off her chin. I was at her side constantly, trying to break through her sadness, trying to give her renewed hope.

Finally one day she turned to me and said, "He's gone."

I wasn't happy with this conclusion. She was hardened with the realization and the finality. She lost the softness and the innocence and optimism I had been able to restore in her, and in fact, in myself. It was as if some light had gone out of her eyes and a deeper, darker glint appeared through which she now saw the world in all its reality. She could no longer see angels. The clouds we once playfully imagined being this or that were now simply clouds. It was as true for the stars as well.

I hated what had happened to her and what was still

happening to her. When I was first starting out in the practice of psychiatry, I used to fixate on the mental problems and see them as small, distorted, ugly creatures. I would focus on killing them, hunting them down through the darkest corridors of a patient's mind, pursuing them relentlessly with my psychiatric weaponry until I had either destroyed them or driven them so far underground, they could do no more serious harm. I hated none as much as I hated the one or ones plaguing Grace, my lovely, wonderful, beautiful Grace.

I know I was a different man at home because of all this, Willow. For the first time my temper was short with Alberta. I had little or no patience for any of her nonsense and everything she was doing those days seemed to me to be bigger and bigger nonsense. It got so she was afraid to come to my office to ask me anything. I would argue with her over trivia. What wasn't trivia to me, however, was her new insistence that we spend a small fortune on upgrading our landscaping. She had brought in a landscape architect who had created a project twice as costly as what the house was probably worth. It envisioned a pond that could qualify as a small lake!

"I can't touch the outside of this precious, historical building, but I can at least improve our grounds," she insisted.

She needed me to convert some investments into liquid cash for her to begin such a project and I resisted. Our normally strained relationship was hanging by threads. I took to spending even more time away from home just so Alberta couldn't harangue me.

As to Grace and her treatments, I did return to the earlier, heavier dosages of her medicine. I hated to do that, but for a while, it seemed to be helping. We spent hours talking about that curse again. The clinic wasn't as sacrosanct as she had come to believe after all. The demon would enter and it would get to me, too. I didn't know at the time, but she already knew she was pregnant and was keeping it a secret just as much because of these troubling ideas as anything else.

*How,* I wondered, *can I turn this around?* Why hadn't I realized how delicate her recovery had been? I began to think that perhaps I was not capable of helping her after all. Maybe Jackie Lee wasn't so wrong. Maybe Grace belonged somewhere else and my keeping her here with me was a purely selfish thing. Maybe I should get her away from me as quickly as I could, I thought.

These questions and thoughts troubled me so much, I know I began to show it in my face. Miles was asking after me constantly. He easily saw the differences in me and was full of concern. When I came home from the clinic, I went right to my office and perused case study after case study trying to find some clues, some technique, some method to make progress with Grace. I often fell asleep in my chair and woke realizing it was the middle of the night.

Obviously, this all had an impact on my relationships and my effectiveness with my other patients, Willow. It occurred to me that Grace might very well be right: my relationship with her was destroying me from within, destroying who I was supposed to be and what I was trained to do. Do you know that for a while there I actually considered the infamous curse?

Like a parasite my frustration fed off of me, draining me, sapping me of my otherwise high-octane energy. Ralston expressed concern and even Nurse Gordon commented about my workload and gave me advice. The irony was the more effort I put into helping Grace, the worse things became because she saw my struggle and my fatigue to be a direct result of my relationship with her. She refused to go on our special walks, and she began to talk more and more about leaving the clinic, claiming it would be better for both of us.

I appealed to her sense of guilt.

"If you do that now," I told her, "I'll feel like more of a failure and instead of helping me, you will hurt me deeply, Grace."

For a while that staved off her talk of leaving. Jackie Lee, however, continued her pressuring, her frequent phone calls, and her threats of simply sending a car and an attorney to pick Grace up. It actually reached the point where my heart would skip a beat whenever I saw a strange automobile make the turn onto our clinic driveway.

And then one night when I was doing everything I could to postpone my returning home, delaying, finding little things to take up my time, just so I wouldn't have to confront an increasingly belligerent Alberta, something terribly explosive occurred. I was making some notes on a report I was completing concerning another patient when Suzanne came running down the corridor to my office. She burst in crying, "Come quickly, Dr. De Beers, something horrible."

"What?" I stood up. "Who is it?"

"It's Grace Montgomery."

My heart did flip-flops. I could feel my legs go numb.

"What happened, Suzanne?" I asked as I followed her out.

"Someone put this on her pillow," she said and pulled the teddy bear's arm out of her uniform pocket. I stopped dead in the hallway and took it from her, turning it in my fingers. Willow, it was as if this toy arm with its stuffing leaking out was a real arm, bleeding in my hand.

"It can't be," I said, shaking my head like one of my own patients going into self-denial. "We looked everywhere."

Suzanne nodded.

The impact of what such a thing might have done to Grace hit me and I charged ahead. I found her sitting as still and as firmly as a statue on her bed, staring at the wall. She had a strange, mad smile on her face, Willow. For a moment she looked so different, it was as if a stranger had wandered into her room.

"I heard her screaming and came quickly," Suzanne said, standing beside me. "I saw the ripped teddy bear arm on the pillow and scooped it off as quickly as I could. That stopped her screaming, but she was as rigid as she is right now, Doctor. It's almost as if she's gone into rigor mortis," she added. "Her arms are locked. I couldn't move her."

I shoved the teddy bear arm into my pocket and approached her. She didn't look at me. Her eyes were so glassy. My biggest fear was she had gone catatonic.

"Grace," I said and reached for her right hand. It was pressed over her left and both were on her stomach. To lift that hand would take some major effort, prying as if with a crowbar. I have seen patients who are in such a catatonic, stiff state, Willow, that forcing their appendages in any direction resulted in actually breaking the bone.

I quickly ordered a sedative and Suzanne went out to get it.

"Grace," I began, "don't do this to yourself. Don't let this happen. We can be strong together. Don't retreat from me, Grace. Stay with me," I pleaded, more like a husband or lover than a doctor. "I need you, Grace. Please."

There was an ever so slight flicker in her eyes that gave me hope. If I could keep this incident to a single reaction of shock, I could keep her from falling into a chronic condition. The nurse returned with the syringe, and I gave Grace the shot. Shortly afterward her body became more pliable, and I was able to get her to lie back.

"Talk to the attendants," I told the nurse. "See if you can learn how this terrible thing happened. Who was in the hallways? Who had access to her room? What did you see?"

"I didn't see anything, Doctor," Suzanne replied, "because I just came on duty a short time ago. Grace must have just pulled the blanket down to prepare for bed when she saw . . . saw it," she told me.

"Okay. I want to be sure there isn't anything else in the room."

I began to search. Nurse Cohen returned with two of our male attendants who joined me, and we examined every inch of the place before determining there was nothing else of any shock value present.

Meanwhile, the nurse checked Grace's pulse and blood pressure. She was resting comfortably, but I decided I would not leave her bedside. I went out and told Miles I was going to remain at the clinic all night. I sent him back to the house for a change of clothing for me, and then I returned to Grace's room and slept in the chair beside her bed, waking every once in a while to observe her. She groaned and moaned a bit, her lips twitching and her eyelids showing rapid eyeball movement. I could just imagine the horrors she was reliving in her deep sleep, and I wished I could somehow crawl into her mind and drive them away.

Just before morning, she woke. I was still sleeping, but I heard her call my name and I opened my eyes. She was on her side, staring at me. I leaped up and knelt beside her bed, reaching for her hands.

"Grace, how are you?"

"I feel so tired, so tired inside," she said.

"I imagine you would. You've been through a terribly traumatic time."

She closed her eyes and seemed to drift off again. I waited. The minutes went by, and then she opened her eyes and looked at me in a strangely cold way.

"I have to leave you, Claude. I have to go away," she said.

I shook my head. "More than ever, you have to stay here now, Grace. I wouldn't let you out. Your mother can bring an army to the door and I'll fight them back."

"I'll destroy you if you don't let me go," she said, then closed her eyes and drifted off again.

This time I let her sleep. I went to my office, got my change of clothing, and went to shower and shave and freshen myself as best I could. I was surprised by Miles's arrival. He came directly to my office to tell me Alberta was very angry.

"I never saw her in such a rage," he said. "After she saw what I was doing and heard you were staying at the clinic. I think she broke something."

"I'll take care of it, Miles. Thank you."

"I thought I'd better let you know," he said and left. There was no doubt in my mind that he would stand beside me on a trip to hell. I was fortunate to have such a dedicated friend and still am. I know he'll always be dedicated to you as well, Willow.

As soon as Nurse Gordon returned to duty, I told her what had occurred and ordered her to conduct a more vigorous investigation.

"Either some attendant is having a sick, jolly time here or we have another patient who is smarter than everyone working here, Nadine. One way or another, I want this brought to an end, a conclusion," I said.

She looked at me and shook her head as if I was the one having delusions. Then she went to carry out my orders.

I returned to Grace's room and found she was more awake, albeit still quite groggy from the medicine and the trauma. I asked one of our female attendants to help her wash and dress, and then I ordered some breakfast for her and had it brought to her room, where I sat with her to make sure she ate something.

"I'm sorry about what happened last night, Grace," I told her. "But I'll not rest until I find out who did that and how. I promise you," I said.

She didn't reply. She ate slowly, her eyes fixed on the floor.

"You've got to help me help you, Grace. I want you to exercise more, take walks again, get back to work in the arts and crafts room, read again, try. If you don't try, you won't get better," I said.

"I've got to leave you, Claude," she repeated, shaking her head. "I've go to go."

"That's silly, Grace. Where will you go? You don't want to return to Florida and to your little boy while you are like this, do you? How will that be for him?"

She pressed her lips together and began to tremble. I put my arm around her shoulders and held her close to me, kissing her cheek and her temple and her hair.

"I won't rest until I help you, Grace. I swear."

"You can't help me," she insisted and then added a cryptic, "I can only help you."

"You can only help me if you get better," I countered. She didn't respond. It was as though she could hear nothing but the voices within her now.

In the days and weeks to follow, her depression was deep again. She had no interest in doing anything but sleeping. I tried to lift her spirits with some mood-enhancing drugs even though I knew this was only a temporary solution, and when I did get her to do something, she did it mechanically without any passion whatsoever.

One afternoon Ralston came to see me to discuss Grace's condition.

"This one is slipping through our fingers, Claude," he began. "Nurse Gordon has been giving me updates on her."

"Giving you updates?"

"Now, don't go chastising her, Claude. She claims you're taking this all too personally, that you've become too involved with this patient to be objective."

"Who is she to make such a diagnosis of the situation, Ralston? That woman steps over the boundaries constantly here. I admit she has a lot of experience and she is very efficient and dedicated, but she is not a trained psychiatrist, and I think it's inexcusable for her to have gone to you like this. I am the lead doctor treating Grace Montgomery, and Nadine knows that. I am disappointed that you even received her, Ralston."

"I'm concerned only for you, Claude," he said.

"You should be concerned only for our patient," I retorted.

"I am. That's why I'm here," he fired back at me.

We were both quiet. It wasn't often that we were at each other like this, and I knew it had a great deal to do with my relationship with Grace.

"Her condition has become very severe. All I'm saying is this might not be the right place for her.

You've had some terrible ups and downs with her, Claude."

"I don't see it that way, Ralston. I think I still have an opportunity to help her. Now, I want you to support me as to this business with Nadine Gordon. It's inappropriate behavior and you would not like it if the roles were reversed," I said firmly.

He nodded. "Okay," he said. "You're not wrong about that."

I called out and asked that Nurse Gordon come to my office immediately. I could see Ralston was uncomfortable, but this was a matter of protocol that I wouldn't permit to be violated.

"Nadine," I began when she entered, "Dr. Price has told me about your reports to him concerning one of my patients. This is entirely inappropriate of you and I resent it," I began.

She raised her shoulders and stiffened her spine.

"I did what I thought was appropriate," she fired back at me.

"You did wrong," I said sharply, "and Dr. Price has remained here to tell you that as well."

Her eyes barely flickered. She didn't as much as glance at Ralston. Her attention was fixed solely on me. I thought she looked disappointed, however, and not angry.

"I was only trying to protect you, Doctor," she said after another moment. "I'm sorry you don't realize that."

"Protect me? From what?"

"From failure," she said. "From making a mistake."

For a moment I didn't know what she meant. What did she know?

"Your motives are admirable, Nadine," Ralston said. "We both appreciate that, but I'm afraid Dr. De Beers is right to be upset. I should have told you to report to him and not to me. I am somewhat at fault here, too, but in the future, please go through the proper channels," he concluded.

"Very well, Doctor," she said. "Is that all?"

"No," I said. Ralston's eyebrows lifted. Nadine's face turned a bit crimson. "How have you been doing with the investigation of the incident in Grace Montgomery's room?"

"The teddy bear's arm?" she asked, as if it was a simple prank someone might pull on Halloween.

"Yes. I consider it quite serious."

"I am confident it has nothing to do with any other patient of ours, Doctor. I can't be sure about all the attendants, but the ones on duty that night are very reliable in my view." She glanced at Ralston. There was something that he hadn't told me. I could see the conspiratorial look.

"And?" I asked.

"And I think there is a possibility Grace Montgomery did this herself."

"That's ridiculous," I snapped back at her.

"You remember Claudia Boston, the teenage girl we had as a patient two years ago?" she said calmly. "She was hiding her own things and accusing everyone of stealing from her."

"That's no analogy. There are too many differences," I said, but Ralston didn't look as if he agreed.

"Nevertheless, it's a possibility, Doctor."

"Well, where did she hide the thing all this time, Nadine?" I asked with exasperation. "We've turned this clinic inside out looking for it, especially in her room."

"Maybe she found a place to hide it during one of your frequent walks with her," she threw back at me.

I know I was the one turning a bit crimson now, Willow. Ralston raised his eyebrows again and gave his "Umm."

"All right," I said. "I don't want to keep you from your duties. Please keep what Dr. Price and I have said to you in mind."

She didn't reply. She just turned and left, but at the door she looked back at me, and Willow, I swear it was a young woman's look of pain. It was as if I had somehow betrayed her and not vice versa.

"Step back a bit, Claude," Ralston told me when he stood up to go. "Take a few deep breaths and look at the situation again. All of it," he added and then left me.

I sat back and gave what he said deep thought. Reviewing my confrontation with Nadine Gordon, however, I was ever more disturbed and concerned. The look I had seen in her eyes when she had left us troubled me. What I suspected, Willow, was that the attention I had been giving to Grace bothered Nadine far too much. It finally occurred to me that in her bizarre fashion, my head nurse was actually jealous. All sorts of thoughts passed through my mind then, and one horrifying one settled at the top.

I deliberately remained at the clinic after Nurse Gordon's shift had ended. As soon as she left the clinic, I went to our nurses' quarters. Everyone was busy attending to her duties. Each of our nurses had her own locker for her private things. I had a master key that opened everything in the clinic, including those lockers. You can't imagine how my fingers trembled when I inserted the key into that lock and opened that cabinet, Willow. At first I saw nothing unusual. Then I moved a blouse aside and there it was: Grace's teddy bear with the arm torn off. I think all the blood in my head went to my feet. I was numb with shock. I took out the stuffed animal, quickly closed the locker, and returned to my office, where I sat trying to decide how to handle this obviously vicious act. The more I looked at the torn teddy bear, the more my shock turned to rage.

I decided not to let another moment go by. I looked at the files, jotted down Nadine's address, and called for Miles.

"I have to make a stop on the way home tonight," I told him and gave him Nadine Gordon's address.

Never having been there before, I searched the directory at the front door and found she was on the first floor. I buzzed and waited. It took so long for her to respond, I didn't think she was home, but finally she asked who it was and I identified myself. The front door was buzzed open immediately, and I heard her open her apartment door down toward the end of the corridor. Wearing a faded pink robe, she was standing in the doorway, obviously quite shocked by my arrival.

"Dr. De Beers, what brings you here?" she asked.

"This," I said and took the torn teddy bear out of my briefcase.

Her face turned a dark shade of crimson.

"Where did you find that?" she demanded.

"Where do you think I found it, Nadine?" I replied and stepped toward her so aggressively, she pulled back. I didn't go any farther into her apartment than her entryway and closed the door behind me. "How could you do such a terrible thing?" I asked.

"I didn't do any terrible thing. I found that and put in my my personal cabinet. I didn't want to disturb you with it," she quicky added. She wasn't a good liar. Her lips trembled too much, her eyes shifted guiltily away from mine.

"You know I won't believe that, Nadine. Why did you do it?"

She looked at me a moment and then shook the fabrications out of her mind and became angry herself.

"Because you were getting too involved with this one patient and you couldn't see what it was doing to you, that's why. She's a conniving, manipulating . . . I did it to help you, to bring about an end to your . . . your . . ."

"What?"

"Fraternizing. You aren't treating her anymore. You're socializing. You're—"

"How dare you do such a thing, assume such things, take such liberties with a patient of mine? This is one of the cruelest things I've seen. I don't want you there any longer, Nadine. I'll send you your severance pay, and I'll have your things sent to you as well. From this day forward you have nothing to do with the clinic or me," I said, turned and opened the door.

"You'll regret that!" she shouted after me. "I am the only one who really cares about you, Dr. De Beers!" she yelled as I walked down the corridor. "You'll see."

I was glad to shut the entrance behind me, take a deep breath, and go on home.

All the confrontation did was fill me with a more desperate determination to be with Grace and to help her. I couldn't wait to get to her the following day. It was a very bright, warm day with streams of thin, sheer clouds spread randomly over the soft blue sky. She had permitted an attendant to take her out to the gardens, where she sat quietly. For a moment I stood back and watched her. She looked so young and innocent, truly part of the natural beauty in which she had surrounded herself, Willow. The breeze made strands of her hair dance softly over her forehead. Two sparrows toyed with landing beside her, bringing a gentle smile to those lovely lips of hers.

When I approached her, she looked up at me. The moment she realized it was I, her eyes became a second or so from filling with tears.

"I'm so happy you've come out here, Grace," I began.

She shook her head. "Let me go, Claude," she pleaded. "Before it's too late."

"What are you talking about, Grace? How can keeping you here with me ever be too late?"

She looked away and took a deep breath.

"Grace, how do you think I would feel the day after you left? How effective would I be with my other patients? Don't you understand? I love you, Grace. You're not simply one of my patients. You're a new reason for me to be, and I hope that somehow I can be the same to you."

She looked up at me, her eyes now awash in those tears I saw pending.

"That can never be, Claude. You know that."

"I don't know anything. I'll find a way. I'll—"

"Claude," she said, pressing her small clenched fists against her bosom. "I'm pregnant."

I could hear the hollow, resonating sound of Nadine Gordon shouting after me in the hallway.

And suddenly it was like all the leaves and blossoms of the flowers around Grace and me came raining down around us like so many tears.

# 10

# A Visit from Jackie Lee

$M$y legs actually went out from under me, Willow. I sat beside her quickly. It was as if a clap of thunder had gone off right beside my ear and snapped me back to reality. This dream I had been living in was over, probably forever. Of course, I asked the expected questions: *Are you sure? When did you realize it?* That was when I figured out exactly when you were conceived. I shook my head, wondering what was wrong with me? How could I have not anticipated this possibility?

"I'm sorry," Grace said.

"Oh, no, no," I protested. "You have nothing about which to be sorry, Grace. I am the one who should have an apology branded on his forehead. I'm your doctor here. You have been under my care."

She stared at me a moment. "You're right," she

said. "I'm not sorry, but not for that reason. I'm not sorry because I am carrying our love inside me," she added.

I felt as if my heart would burst with joy and admiration. How could she, the one who was clinically depressed, the one who had suffered so, be the one to see something beautiful and hopeful in this crisis? Was our love truly that strong? Had I been right to believe in it, in its healing powers?

"That's nice of you to say, Grace," I told her, "but I would be even more remiss if I did not point out the consequences for you as well as for me."

I thought a moment.

"There might be a way to keep people from knowing this. I could contact a doctor I trust and—"

"What are you saying? You can't be serious!" she cried, her eyes wide with shock. "The baby is all we have, can have together."

"That might be true, but . . ."

She shook her head. "I will not have our child destroyed, Claude. Is that what you want?"

"No," I admitted, "but if we reveal what has happened—"

"We won't. We'll find a way. You'll find a way," she insisted. "Promise me, Claude. Promise me you will."

In the face of such determination, I would have promised to pull the moon from the sky.

"Give me some time," I said, and she relaxed and smiled.

Later I was sorry I had made such a promise. No matter how I racked my brain, I couldn't come up with a solution that would leave Grace unscathed, never mind myself. The whole reputation and future of the clinic was at stake as well, Willow. There were dozens of other patients being treated and many waiting for an opening so they could come to our clinic. My staff, Ralston Price, everyone's future were in jeopardy. Ralston had put as much of himself, his time and energy into developing our clinic as I had. How horrible all this would be for him, I thought.

Guilt never weighed down on my shoulders as heavily as it did those days after Grace had confided her situation in me. At home Alberta was becoming more strident, her complaints about our home practically greeting me at the door each and every time I returned. No matter how late the hour, she was at me, telling me how embarrassed she was about our grounds, the poor job the gardeners were doing, the fading paint, the aging driveway, on and on, declaring she was too ashamed of it now to bring any of her friends around.

I wasn't eating well. I lost weight, and when I gazed at myself in the mirror, I saw how gaunt and troubled I appeared. This all reflected on my effectiveness with my other patients, of course. And then there was Grace, looking to me for some solution, her eyes full of confidence and love and expectation. She was more fragile than ever, just teetering on a tightrope of sanity. How much longer did she have before someone else discovered her condition? I had to be careful about her medications, too, and without telling him who she was, confide in a obstetrician friend of mine to be sure I wasn't giving her anything that could harm the fetus.

In the end, Willow, it was your mother, ironically, who moved it all forward, who pushed us into a solution. Once again the patient was the doctor. She quietly took note of the changes in me, the struggle I was undergoing, and on her own, because she was so concerned for me, she decided to take things into her own hands. She didn't tell me what she had done.

One afternoon just before my last therapy session of that day was completed, Edith Hamilton interrupted with a call into my office. Whenever the phone rang and I was with a patient, I knew it had to be something serious and significant or else it had to be Alberta demanding to speak to me.

"I'm sorry, Dr. De Beers," she began, "but Mrs. Montgomery is here and insists on seeing you immediately."

"What?"

She lowered her voice.

"She's going to make a big scene if you don't agree to see her, Doctor. She has a man with her she says is her attorney, too. What should I do?"

"Tell them I will be right with them, Edith," I said. "And tell Nurse Cohen to step into my office."

My heart was thumping so loudly, I thought my patient heard it clear across the room.

"Doctor?" Suzanne said, poking her head around the office door.

I approached her so my patient couldn't hear me.

"Suzanne, I have something of an emergency on

my hands. Could you see that Mr. Winthrop is not unduly agitated by this interruption."

Carlton Winthrop was precisely the wrong patient to be in my office at the moment. He was suffering from acute paranoia and would surely interpret the interruption as some sort of a criticism of him. However, Nurse Cohen was aware of all this and I had confidence she could handle the situation.

As soon as they were gone, I called Edith and asked her to show Jackie Lee and her attorney into my office. Never did my desk seem more like a buffer and fortress than it did at that moment. I was happy to be standing behind it. I smile thinking about it now, Willow, but believe me, I was as close to, as they say, wetting my knickers as ever.

Jackie Lee charged into the office so aggressively, she bumped poor Edith out of her way. The man I assumed to be Jackie Lee's attorney was right on her heels. He was a tall, lean man with very sharp facial features, highlighted by a long, thin nose that looked like he could use it to peck opponents. He carried a briefcase, and held it so closely, it reminded me of a jewel courier with a case containing valuables handcuffed to his wrist.

"Mrs. Montgomery," I said, evincing surprise at her appearance and not daring to refer to her as Jackie Lee at the moment.

Edith lingered curiously in the doorway until my eyes shifted quickly to her. She stepped out and closed the door instantly.

"This," Jackie Lee began, "is my attorney, Mr.

Madison, who served my late husband, Winthrop Montgomery."

I nodded at him, but he didn't say a word, nor did he offer me his hand to shake.

"Please sit down," I said, indicating the sofa.

"I'd rather stand," Jackie Lee said. Her attorney, however, pulled the chair I used when I spoke to my patients, and turned it toward the desk. He offered it to her.

"Go on, Jackie Lee," he said. "This might take a while longer than you anticipate."

"Yes," she agreed. "It might. Thank you, Bennet," she said, and sat. He brought the other chair closer.

"What is this all about?" I asked, lowering myself slowly to my own chair.

"The fact that you don't know what it is all about does not surprise me," Jackie Lee said. She gave her attorney a look of satisfaction and then turned back to me. "My daughter called me this morning, very early, I might add, to tell me she was pregnant," she said.

For a moment I thought my chair had turned to mush and I was actually sinking lower and lower and would disappear from sight. Grace must have come into my office, I thought, and made the call before I had arrived at the clinic.

"You don't look terribly surprised," Jackie Lee said. "Again, I'm not surprised. I imagine such a thing is not unusual here."

I started to shake my head.

"And don't think you can put this all off on someone else. You are the head of this . . . this place. It's your full and complete responsibility."

Had Grace told her everything?

"Of course," I said. "What exactly did Grace tell you?" I asked.

At this point Jackie Lee sat back and her attorney took over.

"Miss Montgomery informed us that she was with child. She said she believed she was raped. She said she believed someone, one of your attendants, perhaps, had come to her room when she was under some sedation or another and taken advantage of her. She has only a vague recollection of this monster, so a clean, precise identification is not possible. Because of her condition, she did not inform her mother, or you apparently, until now, and from what Mrs. Montgomery understands, she is in a late month. She calculates it to be the beginning of the eighth, in fact."

"You would think one of your expert nurses would have noticed," Jackie Lee interjected.

I knew how careful Grace had become when it came to anyone seeing her undressed, and cleverly she had taken to eating more so as to justify the weight gain that had started to be evident in her face. In fact, others on the staff interpreted her new robust appetite as something of a clinical improvement in her condition.

"Nevertheless," Mr. Madison continued, "we are here to produce a solution."

"Don't you have medical doctors examining your patients from time to time?" Jackie Lee snapped at me.

"Well, of course, if a patient has a medical issue, we—"

"A medical issue? What do you call pregnancy, a psychological phenomenon?" she practically screamed.

I stared at her, not moving a muscle, not even a muscle in my face.

"As you can see, this point astounds both of us, Dr. De Beers. Why wouldn't your nurses know she was pregnant?" Mr. Madison asked me.

"Grace isn't incapable of taking care of her own bodily needs, Mr. Madison. She bathes herself, dresses herself. She obviously never indicated—"

"How can she be expected to do that? She's a patient, a mental patient?" Jackie Lee interrupted.

How could I tell her that Grace had been hiding her pregnancy with my blessings all this time?

"Maybe it's not true," I said softly.

The possibility stopped them cold. Jackie Lee, who had been leaning toward me, froze. Then she looked at Mr. Madison.

"You mean, you think Grace Montgomery might be hallucinating this?" he asked.

"It's possible," I offered. I felt very low doing this, Willow, but I also felt so cornered that I had little choice and I was searching desperately for some temporary solution.

Jackie Lee relaxed.

"Well, I will want her examined immediately to determine that," she said.

I nodded. "Absolutely," I said. "Immediately."

"And," she continued, revving up her aggressive

demeanor again, "I want to know exactly what you will do should it be true."

"What I will do?"

"What Mrs. Montgomery means is what we will expect you to do," Mr. Madison said with a cold, wry smile on his thin lips. He opened his briefcase and reached in to produce some papers. "First, we want you to take full responsibility for this event. You will have to have a full investigation of your staff, of course, not only for Miss Montgomery's benefit but for the protection of your other patients."

"Oh, without doubt," I said.

"You will do this all in such as way as to protect Miss Montgomery."

"What he means," Jackie Lee added, "is you won't permit any of this to become public. Should you do so, we will sue you for damages that will turn you into a pauper," she threatened.

"Which brings us to the disposition of the child," Mr. Madison said.

"Child," Jackie Lee said, practically spitting the word on my desk.

"Should the pregnancy continue, of course," her attorney added.

"I see no reason for that to happen," Jackie Lee said. "Who would want such a child anyway?"

"Why don't we wait on that, Mrs. Montgomery? There are medical issues if this pregnancy is as late as you believe it is and—"

"I certainly don't see why Grace would want to give birth to such an thing," she insisted.

"As I said, I need to do a full investigation and—"

"Okay," Mr. Madison said. "Let's look at every contingency here. Should a fetus come to term, you will be responsible for it in every way."

"Absolutely," I said.

"I couldn't imagine bringing such a child back to Palm Beach!" Jackie Lee cried. "No one, no one should ever know about this," she emphasized. "I'm warning you," she continued, pointing her finger at me. "You will be one sorry person should that happen."

Mr. Madison put the documents in front of me on my desk.

"We'll be at the Grand Hotel overnight," he said. "We expect that you will make a full determination of the actuality of the situation, and you will agree and sign to all that we have stipulated here."

"I could sue you and this clinic for thousands and thousands of dollars," Jackie Lee said, her eyes dark and fixed on me, "but that would only bring terrible notoriety to my daughter and to me. I'm sure it would end this . . . this place. You're just lucky about that."

"I'm sorry, Mrs. Montgomery. I will look into it all and get back to you as soon as possible."

"No later than noon tomorrow," Mr. Madison said, as if he was talking about a gunfight.

"Understood," I said.

Jackie Lee opened her purse and took out a handkerchief.

"I feel so guilty. I was the one who put her here," she said, wiping her eyes. "I told her she would be safe, be better off, be helped!"

I couldn't speak, Willow. What was I going to say? That Grace had been helped? That she was better off? In many ways she was. I had confidence that she would be able to return to some sort of a normal life, but my own sense of guilt was so overwhelming, I couldn't utter a sound.

"You will note," the attorney said firmly, nodding toward the papers on my desk, "that Mrs. Montgomery will expect a total refund of all the monies she has spent here."

"Yes," I said, glancing at the documents. "Of course."

"And as soon as she can leave, I want her sent home," Jackie Lee said.

She stood up.

"I want to see my daughter now," she demanded.

"Yes," I said. "I'll see to it immediately." I fumbled for the phone and called Edith.

"Please ask Nurse Cohen to return to my office, or if she's not available, Mrs. Litton," I said.

Nurse Cohen showed up so quickly, I thought she might have been standing just outside my door.

"Nurse Cohen will take you to Grace, Mrs. Montgomery. She should be in arts and crafts, should she not, Nurse Cohen?"

"She should be, but she's not. She's in her room," she replied, her eyes signaling some concern. She turned to Jackie Lee. "I'll take you there."

"Thank you," I said.

As soon as they all left, I felt as if the air had gone out of the room with them. I sat stunned and stared at the closed door. If I didn't know what to do before, I certainly didn't know what I would do now.

I looked over the papers Jackie Lee's attorney had prepared. They detailed everything we had discussed only they also added a financial penalty should I or anyone working at my clinic publicize what had happened to Grace.

While Jackie Lee and her attorney visited with Grace, I sat in my office and stared out my window. Finally, I saw the two of them emerge from the clinic and go to their waiting limousine. After they were driven away, I went to see Grace.

She was sitting in her room, staring out of her window, and turned the moment I entered.

"Grace," I said, shaking my head.

"Don't be angry at me, Claude. I knew you were struggling with a solution, and I was afraid of what you might come to tell me. I made it very clear to my mother: I am having the child, but I had to agree that I would not take him or her back to Palm Beach with me. Otherwise, she vowed she would sue you and the clinic and make a big issue of it all. She would because she believes at that point it would make no difference. My bringing home the child will ruin her, as well as me, she claimed. I have no doubt she was serious about that, Claude. I'm sorry. In my desperation, I have only made things worse."

"No, no," I said. "Don't think that. Don't ever think that."

"What will we do?"

"There has to be a way for us. . . ."

"Oh, Claude, you of all people should not live in any fantasy. Even after a significant period of time, if we should somehow be together with the child, people will know. You would be ruined. The clinic would be seriously damaged. I couldn't live happily with that sort of guilt."

I nodded and smiled at her. How wonderful she was, Willow. How wise and strong when she had to be strong for us. It was never as clear to me as it was then that your mother would find her way in this world, that she didn't need to be in any sort of institutional environment. In a strange and beautiful way, our love, her pregnancy had brought her up from the depths of the darkness that had brought her here.

I knelt at her feet and put my head gently against her stomach. I could feel you kicking inside, Willow, and I lifted my tear-filled eyes and looked at Grace.

"The baby knows its father," she said softly.

I made Grace a promise then. I told her that some-how, someway our baby would be with me. Again, I had no idea how I would accomplish this, Willow, but in your mother's presence, with her smile branded in my brain, I knew in my heart that I would find the way.

When I returned to my office, Ralston was waiting for me. I closed the door behind me and he looked up.

"What's going on, Claude?" he asked. "I heard about the Montgomery woman showing up here with an attorney. Does it have anything to do with Nadine Gordon leaving so abruptly?"

I had kept the entire teddy bear incident from him, not wishing to open a new can of worms. As far as everyone knew, Nadine had left entirely of her own accord. It was my feeling that she would have anyway, once she had seen how I had taken her actions and how I now felt about her and her work.

"No, Ralston," I replied.

"Well, then, what did they want, Claude?" he asked.

"You had better sit, Ralston," I said.

He did just that.

And I told him, Willow. I told him everything.

# 11

# A Little Invasion

To my surprise, Ralston wasn't all that surprised. He had developed suspicions for some time, but, as he said, he had hoped I would come to my senses.

"Now that I see how you are taking all this and how disturbed you are, I see that you would never have come to your senses, Claude," he told me. "You're actually head over heels."

I assured him I would do everything possible to protect our clinic, even if it meant taking some great financial loss to myself. In turn he assured me that he wasn't as concerned about anything as he was about me.

"You're far too valuable and talented a psychiatric therapist to throw it all away, Claude. Your patients and your future patients would be the losers. I'll stand by you and do whatever we have to do," he promised.

We hugged each other. His loyalty and devotion to me only made me feel worse, Willow. I phoned Mr. Madison at his hotel and told him that Grace was pregnant, of course, and that I would sign their documents and follow their wishes. He was coming by in the morning to pick them up. Jackie Lee would not return, he said. She was too upset to see her daughter in this environment. He did say she did not want to have Grace sent back to Palm Beach until it was all over, and the veiled threat added was if she was worse, or would give Jackie Lee any new problems, he would be making another visit to the clinic to see me.

Miles took one look at me on the way home that night and saw the turmoil raging inside me. He thought it was all because of Alberta and her constant nagging about the house and her loss of social standing. She had been particularly difficult during the past two months, and our maid and cook had quit. Miles deliberately took every detour he could in the house and on the grounds to avoid her, but he wasn't deaf to the shouting and complaining. He had a bit of a dry sense of humor about it, telling me that "Mrs. De Beers took her first step toward firing another maid today. She hired her."

I was in so desperate a state of mind during our ride home that I didn't realize we were there until Miles turned off the car engine.

"You all right, Dr. De Beers?" he asked, turning to me. I was just sitting there in the rear seat staring at my thoughts.

"What? Oh. Yes, Miles, thank you," I said and

stepped out. It wasn't until I was about to open the front door that the whole plan came to me, Willow. Sometimes it isn't until the final moments that we find solutions. The prospect of that great chasm before us makes us churn our brains and search our hearts with the power of the survival instinct, I guess.

Alberta was upstairs in her room. So that I would know what was happening that night, she had taped the invitation to the mayor's ball, a charity event, on the balustrade. I couldn't miss it the moment I started up the stairs. If I was ever not in the mood to go to one of her affairs, it was tonight, I thought, but with every step I took, I went farther and farther out on thin ice.

I paused at her door a moment, questioning my ability to do what I had decided. If I couldn't do this from the very beginning, I thought, I certainly couldn't carry it forward afterward, when it was most necessary to wear the masks and take on the behavior dictated by the fabrications I was about to create.

I knocked on her door, and a moment later she responded. I entered her bedroom. In her robe and slippers, she was sitting at her vanity table toying with some new way to set her hair. Her face was covered in one of those special, expensive creams she bought to keep wrinkles from forming and her skin from being anything but alabaster. I was never able to look at her when she performed these rituals to whatever goddess of beauty she worshiped and not laugh to myself at how comical she appeared. She went from mud packs, to milk and herbal coatings, wore cucumbers on her eyes, and even had a mix that included skunk oil.

Alberta had her own personal complexion expert the same way some people had personal trainers, and this person always seemed to come up with some new discovery. Of course, each one was more expensive than the former.

She turned in her chair and looked at me. For once, she was able to see past herself and really read my mood.

"What's wrong now, Claude?" she asked.

I closed the door slowly, dramatically, behind me and went to the dressing bench at her bed.

"My goodness, what happened now?" she cried. "Did one of your troubled patients commit suicide or something? Is there going to be a scandal in the paper? What?"

"There could be a scandal," I began. This was where my strength with her lay. This was the only way to get her to care, I thought. "But I have a way to prevent it, I believe. I will need your full cooperation, however."

Her eyes, mere dark pools within those layers and layers of cream, somehow deepened and widened with surprise. She began to wipe off the cream.

"What happened?" she demanded.

"We've had something of an incident at the clinic," I said. "Apparently, one of our attendants has impregnated a patient."

"Impregnated a patient? You mean, raped a woman?"

I nodded.

"Can't you speak plainly and simply, Claude? Well,

what is the problem? Have someone come in and give her an abortion," she said.

I shook my head.

"Can't be done. It's far too late, and there are other complications, complications for the patient," I added before she could ask.

"Too late. You mean no one noticed this patient was pregnant for months and months and months?"

"Yes, that's it, Alberta."

She stared at me.

"As it turns out, Alberta, this patient happens to be the daughter of a very wealthy, powerful woman who, with her attorney, could create great problems for the clinic and . . . for us," I said.

I could hear her take a very deep breath. She brought her hand to her heart and sat back against the vanity table.

"For us?"

"Well, of course. I'm the head doctor, Alberta. Everything reflects on me no matter what."

"What about Ralston? Why isn't it just as much his fault?" she asked, now wiping her face more vigorously.

"That doesn't help us, Alberta. Of course he would share the responsibility, as you say."

"His wife isn't as involved in society. She doesn't do anything. It won't matter to her nearly as much," Alberta complained.

"Exactly."

"Well, what are you going to do, Claude? Will it be in tomorrow's papers?"

"No. It won't be in any papers ever if we handle it the way I want to handle it, Alberta."

"And what way is that, Claude?" she asked, her face now cleared of the cream.

"I can keep the baby's birth relatively unknown. I'll conduct my own private and quiet investigation in the clinic as to who is responsible."

"Good," she said. "Then you can solve the problem."

"Well, not quite," I said. "I would like to adopt the baby, like us to adopt the baby," I corrected.

Her mouth came unhinged.

"You and I have not been able to have our own child, and I thought—"

"Are you mad? Are you as crazy as the people you treat in that nuthouse? Adopt a crazy woman's baby!"

"She's not a crazy woman, Alberta. She is someone who suffered from acute depression, but she is well on her way to being healthy enough to go home and—"

"So let her take the baby home, too."

"Her mother won't permit that, Alberta, and she has the wherewithal to carry out any threats she makes, believe me," I said, imposing a heavy, dark look on my face to impress her.

She thought a moment and then shook her head.

"Then give the baby away, to some adoption agency. It's as simple as that."

"No, we can't take that chance, Alberta. In this day and age people can find their origins. Whoever adopts the baby will have a right to know where the child came from, especially if it came from a clinic like mine. There could be an even bigger scandal if we were caught doing that. It could blow up in our faces, and then where would we be? When you lose control of the situation, you take a bigger chance."

"I won't do it. I won't have a crazy child brought up as our own."

"There's nothing wrong with the child, Alberta. The problem the woman suffers comes from behavioral, social problems, not genetic," I said.

"Don't give me that medical gobbledygook, Claude. A disturbed person is giving birth to a . . . a what? Is it a boy or a girl?"

"We don't know that yet, Alberta, but I assure you there is nothing mentally wrong to be inherited."

She shook her head. "It's too late for us, Claude. I'm not suited to be a mother now. I can't raise an infant, especially not my own. I won't do it. Find another solution," she ordered and turned back to her vanity mirror.

"I have some ideas, Alberta. Just listen," I pleaded.

She didn't respond. She went about her cosmetics as if I was already gone.

"I will hire a nanny immediately who will be solely responsible for the child. You won't have an iota of work in that regard."

"Ridiculous."

"She and I will be solely in charge of the infant's upbringing."

"What is this?" she asked, turning back to me. "Some sort of psychological study you want to do?"

"Yes," I said. "In a way that's true."

She stared a moment, thinking.

"People will admire you for this, Alberta. What a great act of charity to be performing, adoption. You will just have to keep the child's origins to yourself."

"Who would want to admit to having the child of a nutcase?" she fired back. She was still shaking her head. "I can't imagine it. I just can't."

"We would improve the house, of course, fix up a nursery, prepare quarters for the nanny . . ."

She turned to me again, her eyes narrowing. "Improve the house? Does that include my landscaping designs?" she asked.

"If you think that's absolutely necessary, I suppose . . ."

"Absolutely necessary? What do you think I've been shouting about all these months? Of course it's absolutely necessary. Have we had a dinner here recently? No. And you know why, Claude. I've been too embarrassed about our grounds to have any distinguished guests come here."

"I understand," I said. I felt as if my arm was being so twisted behind my back, I could do nothing but surrender to every demand she would make.

She sat there, considering. "You will hire someone who will be completely responsible for the child? I will have nothing to do with caring for this . . . infant?"

"Just as I said, yes."

"And we'll get started immediately on all the improvements?"

"I would want them done in time for the child's arrival here, yes."

She thought again. "I suppose we could make some sort of social announcement about it, about the need to adopt needy little babies. There is Clair Softer's child welfare organization, the one that holds that auction dinner every year at the Ritz."

"Oh, I'm sure you can do something significant with all that, Alberta," I said quickly.

"Don't patronize me, Claude," she fired back, her face screwed tightly. "Don't think I don't see how you are manipulating me here."

"I'm—"

"That's okay," she continued. "I'll let you manipulate me as long as I get what I want. I just knew that clinic of yours would be the death of us. You can't spend your entire life around disturbed people day and night and not be damaged in some way or another. Why can't you simply have a practice like some of your colleagues and work a nine to five office with weekends off and vacations and—"

"Maybe someday, Alberta," I said to stop her.

She looked at me and shook her head. "No, Claude, you'll never do it. All right," she said with a deep sigh, "I'll agree under the conditions you have outlined and promised. What I will expect from you now is a lot more attention to my needs, however. I am tired of showing up to my affairs without my husband, the distinguished doctor, at my side."

"I understand," I said. She didn't know it, but there was practically nothing I wouldn't have agreed to do that night.

"Good," she said. "Good. Well, go on, get ready. We

have an important occasion to attend this evening," she ordered.

Why was it when I stood up and left that bedroom that night, Willow, that I felt as if I had just made a pact with the devil?

When I told Grace, she was ecstatic, of course. I left out all the promises and stipulations I had made with Alberta, and I made it sound more like Alberta was positive and encouraging. Why give Grace any more to worry about? I thought.

"Oh, Claude, at least our child will be with you," she said. "How wonderful."

"That way, Grace, you will always be with me, too," I said, "and in time—"

"Let's not talk about anything else just yet, Claude," she said. "Let's just take it all a step at a time. Please," she begged. "No fantasies for now."

I laughed and agreed.

Six weeks later you were born, Willow. Grace and I had sat many nights discussing what we would name you if you were a girl, and she thought naming you after the clinic itself was a wonderful idea.

"It ties the baby even closer to us," she said.

She was seeing so many things faster and clearer than I was those days. I was still tiptoeing around Alberta, terrified that she would somehow change her mind. To ensure she didn't, I moved quickly on renovations, each major change and expense locking up our deal more tightly. She didn't miss a chance to complain in advance, of course, making me promise to get rid of you should you prove to be a psychologically ill child.

In the meantime I concentrated on finding your nanny. Obviously, she had to be a very special person, Willow. She had to be someone in whom I could confide. Whoever it was, she was sure to see Alberta's indifference to the infant, and in time would surely realize the complexities of our situation. She had to be someone who could tolerate Alberta, too. So you see, this was to be a very difficult search.

Ralston helped me here. His wife, Palma, was Portuguese and had relatives in Brazil. An aunt of hers had a friend who wanted to come to America. Her name was Isabella Martino, the woman you would come to call Amou because she used the Portuguese phrase *Amou Um* whenever she spoke to you, a phrase that meant "loved one." How lucky I was to find her, Willow.

I arranged for her trip to America and, through some influential friends of mine in the government, made it possible for her to stay here and work for us. As soon as I met her, I liked her. You never knew this, but I had her meet your mother just before you were born.

We didn't tell Isabella everything immediately. I was afraid that the weight of such information might frighten her off. It turned out to be an unnecessary fear. No one could have handled it all as well as your wonderful Amou did. She understood everything quickly, and nothing more quickly or more deeply than she understood Grace's love for me and mine for her. Later, some time after that one and only meeting she had with Grace with me present, of course, she told me she knew then, just by the way we looked at each other, and spoke to each other that we were the parents of the child.

I began by telling Amou all the things I had told Alberta. She accepted it. She would believe anything I wanted her to believe. That was clear. The most emotionally nervous time for me was the first time I introduced her to Alberta. I had told Alberta that I believed I had found a wonderful nanny. She had little interest in whether the nanny was as good for the child as I said she was. She couldn't have made that any clearer to Amou than she did that first meeting at our home.

After I showed Isabella where her quarters would be and where the nursery was, right next to her room with an adjoining door, I introduced her to our current household help, Miles in particular. I could see he liked her very much. Later, of course, Amou would take over more of the household chores, especially the cooking. Alberta, despite herself, liked Amou's cooking, and Amou quickly learned how to handle your stepmother.

"You understand," Alberta told her during that first meeting, "that you will be totally in charge of this infant. You won't have much time off. The only way you will be able to have a day off is if Claude finds a suitable baby-sitter. I am far too busy to have any of those responsibilities."

"I have no place to spend a day off, Mrs. De Beers," Isabella told her. "This home, these grounds are so beautiful, I will enjoy my free time here, I'm sure."

"Yes, well, the grounds weren't always as beautiful as they are now," Alberta made a point of telling her, glaring at me at the same time. "I am still in the process of completing the project."

"You are doing some job," Isabella said. "There are beautiful gardens around some magnificent estates in Brazil that don't compare."

"Well, I'm glad someone can come here and immediately appreciate my efforts. If you have any problems with the baby, medical or otherwise, you will call my husband to discuss them. You understand that?"

"*Si.* Yes," Isabella said, glancing at me. We had already discussed all that, and I had prepared her for Alberta's indifference.

"It's very important that the child be kept from my guests whenever I have a dinner party. I don't want some screaming infant tearing their attention away."

"*Eu compreendo,*" Isabella said.

"What?"

"Oh, I'm sorry. I forget sometimes and speak Portuguese. It means I understand, Mrs. De Beers."

"Great. I don't know a word of Portuguese, Claude."

"As you can see, Alberta, Isabella speaks English. It's understandable she would slip into her own language occasionally."

"Well, whenever you talk to me, make an effort not to do that," she ordered Isabella.

"*Si.* I mean yes, Mrs. De Beers."

"*Si* is okay," Alberta relented. "It's very common to hear that these days with all the Spanish and Mexican people around us, but other than that—"

"I understand," Isabella said, this time with some emphasis.

It brought a slight smile to my lips that Alberta did not catch.

"Well, all right," she said, waving her hand at me, "you're my husband's employee. Just remember that. When do you expect this little invasion to occur, Claude?" she asked, and I gave her my estimate.

"I'll never get used to it," she vowed and left us.

Isabella looked at me with those dark, wise eyes of hers you will never forget. We exchanged so much without speaking.

She was there at your birth, Willow. You went from your mother's arms to hers and the love that bonded them forever passed through you to each of them. I witnessed it and felt it and so did Grace.

Afterward, we held on to each other and she wept softly. My heart was so torn, I didn't think I would have the strength to leave her. I had to, of course, and it took all of my powers to stop thinking about her alone, without the child she had just birthed, your beautiful little face gone from her eyes. She had held you and studied you like someone who knew she had to memorize every part of you to hold you again in her heart.

Amou and I brought you home that night. Alberta never came downstairs to look at you. She was preparing for a meeting of her Woman's Club. I told her you were there in the nursery.

"I hope I don't hear any wailing in the middle of the night," she said.

"You won't," I promised.

Then I went downstairs to the nursery and sat

beside you while you slept, and I wondered when you would know the truth of your birth and if you would ever feel it before I had told it to you.

As I sit here writing all this now, I think about the times I felt your eyes on me and the times I had your full story on the tip of my tongue. I have always been afraid of what the weight of all that truth would do to you. I know how you have suffered with Alberta's ranting about your origins, and I have often assured you that what she says is not true. I must confess that Amou does a better job of it than I do. As more and more time passed, I felt myself moving further and further away from the opportunity or the chance to tell you everything. I have guarded your mother and my secrets closely for many reasons, Willow, not the least of which remains my terrible sense of guilt.

For I permitted her to leave you and for that and all that followed, I will forever be ashamed.

# 12

# Mommy

Now that Jackie Lee had what she wanted, she wasn't all that eager for your mother to return to Palm Beach. She wanted assurances that Grace would not be too much of a problem for her to handle. Her questions were always weighted with underlying threats.

"If she's worse because of what happened there, you will hear from Mr. Madison," she told me repeatedly.

I had to confide in Grace about it.

"I'll deal with my mother when I go home," she said. "Don't worry about her anymore, Claude."

She remained at the clinic for a while. Every day I would bring her news about you, and I started to bring her pictures as well. To her credit she was thinking more and more about Linden then, too. Your birth had brought back the memories of him, and she began to miss him more. I felt sorry for her, for how she was so torn between going home to her little boy and staying at the clinic to be close to me and to you. There was never any question about where she would end up, not now, not after all we had arranged.

All of her traumatic experiences matured Grace dramatically. The therapist in me saw the changes clearly. Some pleased me, but some saddened me, for she had become someone who now accepted whatever Fate decided. I suppose what pleased me was her strength, her quiet resolution. Sadness and disappointment would not have their way with her anymore. She was what anyone would call a wiser woman.

What I missed, of course, was the innocent, childlike view of the world, those trusting eyes that would settle on me with a soft smile of contentment around them. Now she looked at me as if from a great distance. Every minute, every hour that passed lengthened the distance we knew would come between us.

I had reduced her medications while she was pregnant, and now she was practically weaned off them entirely. She spent her time walking and reading, working in the arts and craft center and talking to other patients in a way that made the more nervous and high-strung ones calmer. It got so many looked forward to seeing her, and on a few occasions I viewed her actually doing better than my trained staff and nurses when it came to settling down a patient who was acting out. Half jokingly, I told her she should consider a career in mental health.

"I've had a career in mental health," she replied. "Enough to last a lifetime, Claude."

Ah, yes, I thought, how true.

We still took our walks occasionally, only now they were slower, both of us more pensive. Paragraphs and paragraphs of dialogue between us no longer had to be said. We were that good at reading each other's thoughts, sensing each other's moods.

At home Alberta continued her aloof attitude toward the baby. There were times I believed she really had forgotten you were there, Willow. I would see this sudden look of surprise when you cried out or when Amou walked through a room holding you or took you out in the carriage. When our dinner and party guests asked about you, she would unabashedly tell them to ask me.

"The child is Claude's project," she would say, as if I were running some sort of experimental laboratory in the house and doing research on child behavior.

One night at dinner she did ask me about Grace. It wasn't so much a question as it was a demand.

"I suppose you should tell me about the infant's mother now, Claude."

"What do you want to know?"

"Everything, of course. And don't give me any of that gobbledygook about patient-doctor confidence or something," she added firmly.

Alberta, I decided, would have made a wonderful cross-examiner at the Nuremberg Nazi trials.

"I told you already. She was a young woman who suffered acute depression. I treated her with medication and therapy counseling. In time we worked out her problems and she has become a much stronger person. I have no doubt she will do well in the outside world."

"Then she's gone?" she asked.

I thought for a moment and decided it would be better all around if that was what Alberta believed.

"Yes, she's gone."

"Do you think there is any possibility that in the foreseeable future she would want her own child?" she asked.

Of course, it was a question I had lodged in the darker closets of my own mind. Would there be a time when Jackie Lee would agree to such a thing? How long would it be before that occurred? If it was too long, it would be difficult, if not emotionally and psychologically damaging to you, Willow. I had to consider all that.

"No, Alberta," I said. "I don't believe that will ever happen."

"I don't see why not. Aren't mothers supposed to want their own offspring, Claude? Something more must be wrong with this person if that's the case. Maybe you've missed something, something that can be inherited and now we'll be the ones suffering with it," she pointed out.

"Most unlikely, Alberta," I insisted.

"Most unlikely, Alberta," she mimicked. "The know-it-all, great doctor. Well, I predict otherwise, Claude De Beers, and when my prediction comes true, I want more than an apology from you. I want you to agree to send her away to some sort of institution for such children."

"That, Alberta, I will never do," I said. I said it with such conviction that even she was taken aback. "How would it look if I, the head of a nationally reputable mental clinic, couldn't handle his own problems?" I added to soften my sternness.

It gave her some pause, and she pulled herself back and began to eat again, stopping only to say, "I hope that you're right."

However, it was a theme Alberta would not put aside, Willow. Up until now, the time I am writing this, you have experienced some of it yourself. I remain hopeful that these tensions in the home will dwindle, thin out, and dissipate, but who can tell? What I do know is everything I've learned and all my insight and skill tells me you will be a wonderful young woman soon, bright, personable, and, I must say in all modesty, a very beautiful woman, too. You take after your mother, there.

I was never going to be the one to tell her it was time for her to go home. She knew that. We skirted that discussion often during the time she spent at the clinic after your birth. Jackie Lee called periodically. She claimed she had begun to prepare Linden for the revelations to come. I, of course, was skeptical of that and even more afraid for the child. This was not something anyone could just drop on a child one day and expect all to be well. I warned Grace about that.

"Your experiences here might come in handy back in Palm Beach, Grace," I told her. "Linden will have some problems with all this."

"I know. This is why I think it's time for me to go,

Claude. The sooner I can get back there and be with him, the better it will be. I'm sure you agree about that."

"Yes," I said. "I do, but I don't want to," I added, and she smiled.

We were walking along the path that led us down to the river and then over to the clearing where we had made love that wonderful warm afternoon. We sat and listened to the water and watched the birds who always seemed so busy around us.

"Maybe they're talking about us," I said. "Maybe they're telling other birds who will tell other birds until all the birds back in Palm Beach know the story of us, too."

"Why, Dr. De Beers, such romantic fantasy, and from a world-renowned psychiatrist, a man of science," she teased.

"If all we have is our science, our chemicals, and our laws of Nature, Grace, we're truly deprived. Beauty is indefinable and not something we can create in a test tube, nor is love," I said. "Nor is love."

Her eyes glassed over with tears, and she turned away from me and pulled her knees up like she used to when we had first taken these therapeutic walks together. She looked like a little girl again, and just for a few moments, we were both like teenagers, discovering each other, discovering the best in ourselves. I kissed her and held her. We remained that way for a long time. We were actually out there until the sun began to sink behind a row of trees and it grew cooler.

"We had better go back," I said.

For a while we walked holding hands, and then, when the clinic came into view and others could see us, I let her go. I felt as if she was already drifting away from me then, and my heart ached, Willow.

The next day she called Jackie Lee, and then Jackie Lee phoned me and I told her yes, it was time for Grace to go home. She would be fine now.

"I hope so," Jackie Lee said.

That night I took another picture of you, Willow, and then I brought it back to the clinic and gave it to your mother. Some time later she sent me a box. Fortunately, Alberta didn't see it arrive. When I opened the box, I found a doll she had made, the face so clearly modeled after yours. I put it away to save for you. She used the pictures of you well.

I tried to keep myself occupied the day your mother left the clinic, but it wasn't working. She was waiting for the car to arrive to take her to the airport. Jackie Lee had made the arrangements and wasn't coming to escort her.

"If she can't come home herself, she is certainly not ready to come home," she declared. In a sense she was right about that. I had no doubt Grace could do it anyway.

Finally I went to her room. I could see in her face that she had been hoping I wouldn't.

"I don't want to say goodbye, Claude. If you've come here to do that . . ."

"No, not goodbye. I'm here to be sure everything is fine. I do that with any patient I've released," I said.

"You're not a good liar, Claude De Beers," she said.

"Despite all your talents, you can't do that well. At least not when your heart isn't in it."

I laughed and went to her window to look out. How many hours had she spent here? I thought, gazing at this scene. It wasn't something she would soon forget.

"Remember when I first came here, I asked you who had been in this room before me?"

"Yes," I said.

"What will you say when someone new comes and is assigned to this room?"

"I'll say a wonderful, beautiful person came through this clinic and taught me far more than I taught her. I'll say she's left me, but she's not gone."

"You might frighten the new patient saying things like that."

"I doubt it. I mean that, Grace. You're not going to be gone, not ever."

She smiled at me with that new, wise look of hers that made me feel more like the patient being humored.

"Listen to me," I said, seizing her hands in mine. "Some day I'm going to come to you. I'll charter a boat and I'll come sailing into that little harbor of yours. I'll come at night, so look for me. It will be a surprise. One day, one night, I'll just be there."

"Do you want me to believe that, Claude? Do you really want me to have that hope?"

"Yes," I said.

I regretted saying that almost immediately after I did, Willow. It was selfish of me. I was asking her to wait for me, not to fall in love with anyone else, to believe in some romantic miracle. I knew always that the more time that passed, the more impossible that would be. There were too many other people to consider, not least of all you.

"Take care of our little Willow," she said. "And when it's the best time for it, Claude, and not a moment sooner, tell her about us. Promise me you will, but promise me you will use your skill and your expertise in deciding when that should be."

"I promise, Grace," I said.

I kissed her and held her in my arms for the last time. There was a knock on the door. Edith Hamilton had come to let us know Grace's limousine was here and the driver was waiting for instructions.

I carried her small suitcase myself and walked her to the limousine. Edith had a beautiful bouquet of red roses for her.

"To wish you the best of luck, my dear," she said. They hugged.

Ralston came out to wish her well, and then the whole day staff, all the attendants and nurses who had grown to admire her, came to hug her and kiss her and wish her well. She was crying now, but avoiding my eyes.

Remember I told you about the day she arrived? How I could recall every detail of it? It was the same the day she left, Willow. It was partly cloudy, but the sun was strong, and when it could peak down between clouds, it sent a shaft of light that chased away shadows and darkness and filled our hearts with promises.

Grace got into the limousine. I held the door open

and told the driver I would close it. He could get into the car and start the engine. He did so and I stood there looking in at her.

"I'll be on the dock with a lantern swinging from my hand," she said, "to guide you to my waiting arms."

She turned away and I closed the door. It felt as if it had shut on my heart, Willow. The limousine started away, and I followed it down the driveway a bit and then stood there watching until it disappeared around the turn and was gone.

I couldn't go right back into the clinic. Instead, I walked and stood for a while under one of our great willow trees. I had to get hold of myself. I had a patient to see in less than an hour, and then we were having a staff conference later. My life wouldn't permit me to take too much time to mourn my tattered heart. I wandered about for a while, thinking.

Finally I felt strong enough and I walked back. I saw Ralston watching me from the window of his office. The concern in his face helped me get a firmer hold of myself. Later that evening I spent a good half hour at your crib watching you sleep, studying your face, seeing Grace in you.

Amou came by and stood beside me.

"This child," she said. "She will be a beautiful young woman like her mother and wise like her father."

I didn't have to answer. She saw the hope in my eyes and she smiled. I knew then how close you two would become, and I was so grateful for that.

Along with the doll your mother sent us, there was a letter. I was so silly about it, Willow. I didn't open it for days and days. She had sent me a short letter earlier to assure me she was fine, but this one, because it was with the doll, carried some special meaning for me. Every time I went to open it, my fingers trembled so, I had to stop. Finally, one rainy night after I had been home a while and you were asleep and Alberta had gone to bed, I went to my office and sat staring out the window, listening to the drops tap on the glass.

I reached into my drawer and took out the letter and then finally I opened it.

*Dearest Claude,*

*I struggled for a while trying to think of something I could give Willow. I thought about writing a long letter you would give her someday. I thought about pictures, but then, I found myself working on this, and it seemed the best possible gift I could give her. Please explain that for me when the time comes.*

*I'm doing better and better with Linden. Taking your advice, I've moved slowly, carefully, letting him grow with the truth. He's very artistic, too. I can't believe what he can do at his young age, and he loves working in the sand and creating things.*

*My mother is much better. She's settled into her new lifestyle well, and she is enjoying society again. The people who have rented our estate and who live in the big house are so occupied with their social life, they don't seem to notice Linden and me very much. It's actually more beautiful here for me than it ever was. I enjoy my long walks on the beach with Linden. It's so quiet at times, I feel as if we are on our own island.*

*I'm getting stronger and stronger every day, and I no longer have any fears about myself. Every once in a while I think about my daddy, but not like I used to. He's not walking on the beach or beckoning me to follow him anywhere, so don't be afraid of that. I think about his smile, his confident stride, his loving kisses and hugs, and all of the dreams he had for me. I have come to where I can cherish memories without them harming me or giving me such great pain, I can't breathe. You helped me get to this point, Claude. You really are a wonderful doctor, and I know you will help so many, many more people in your wonderful clinic. I could never feel good pulling you from that. A parade of troubled souls would haunt me.*

*Yet, I would be less than honest if I didn't tell you I dream our dream. We can have fantasies without them damaging us. You taught me that, too, Claude; or, perhaps as you say, I taught you.*

*Occasionally, just to please myself and to keep you thriving in my heart, I go out to our dock at night. Don't feel bad about that, either. It's good for me. Really.*

*I go out there, Claude, and I look out at the darkness and the sea and I wave a lit lantern.*

*I imagine you coming.*

*I imagine you stepping off that boat and me rushing into your arms.*

*And I imagine you've brought a little girl along. She waits patiently. You step aside and she looks at me and without a bit of prompting, she says, "Mommy."*

*What a wonderful word that is, Claude.*

*What a wonderful gift.*

*And you've given it back to me.*

*After all this, you've given it back to me.*

> *Love forever and ever,*
> *Grace*

# DARK SEED

# 1

# Early Days

The flash of light above me on my ceiling and the boom that followed snapped my eyes open. The sound of my own scream was so shrill, it seemed to be coming from outside me. It made me shrink and close up inside myself until I was like someone cowering deep down in the protective world of a bomb shelter, waiting for the explosions above to end.

For as long as I could remember, I believed the thunder and lightning that crashed and sizzled in the dark South Carolina summer skies could come right into our house. I imagined that terrible fear began the first time I was woken as an infant, shaken out of sleep by a loud clap and a flash of light on the ceiling of my nursery. I screamed then, just as I was screaming and crying now, even though I was already ten years old. Because my nanny Amou slept downstairs, tucked away in a small room as far from my mother as possible in our estate home, she did not hear my wails of fright.

But then again, she didn't have to hear them to know they were coming. No one in my life would ever be as sensitive to and aware of my feelings as Amou was. The moment she heard the thunderstorm begin, she knew I would be afraid, and she began to make her way quickly through the kitchen, down the corridor, and up the stairs to comfort me, but also to make sure I did not disturb my mother—which was unlikely, since she slept with earplugs.

My mother slept with earplugs because she claimed my father snored loudly enough to wake the dead. She was very protective of her sleep, asserting it was essential not only for good health, but for healthy skin. So she did not hear my cries very often, but even if she had, she would not have come to comfort me, and she would have certainly complained if my father had risen, put on his robe and slippers, and come to my bedside. Although he could tiptoe and move with great care, he could or would disturb her, and that would bring on another and perhaps more horrifying crash of thunder and flash of lightning in our home.

"Isabella will take care of her," she would tell him if he dared stir. "That's why we hired the woman. I am not one of those wives who cleans her home before the maid arrives. What is the point of having servants if you don't let them serve, especially a nanny, to take away the burden of raising a child, especially *this* child?"

I often heard her discussing me with my father, not that she cared if I did or didn't hear. She certainly spoke loudly enough, her voice barely muffled by the walls between rooms. In fact, I never heard her whisper in our home. The only time she actually lowered her voice was when she was speaking to me and wanted to impress me with something.

"It's not natural for a girl that age still to be afraid of such things," she declared after she heard me crying once. "I'm not the psychiatrist, Claude. You are, and the irony here is that you can't see she's not normal."

My mother made that statement so often that it became the mantra in our home. I could hear it echoing through the house, whispered in the shadows: "She's not normal. She's not normal."

I couldn't help but wonder if it wasn't so, especially after I was force-fed the truth.

"Everyone has fears, Alberta," my father explained to her patiently. There was no one I knew who spoke and conducted himself with as much control. His anger was kept hidden under blankets and blankets of psychological techniques. However, my mother even complained about that.

"I feel like I'm living with a Jehovah's Witness. You slam the door in his face and all he says is 'Have a nice day.'"

Nevertheless, no matter how calmly and reasonably he responded to her complaints, she insisted she was right about me.

"Everyone does *NOT* have fears like this child," she asserted, and waved off any argument or logic he might offer. Sympathy for me was simply not in the cache of emotions she carried in her cold heart. I had no idea why, but I did blame myself and tried as hard as I could to do things that would please her. I never seemed to be successful.

There was no more comforting sight to me anyway than Amou standing in my bedroom doorway.

"Hush, hush, Amou Um," she urged when she came to my bedside during the thunderstorm. Amou was a forty-three-year-old Portuguese woman my parents had hired right after I had been born. *Amou Um* was a Portuguese expression for "loved one," which was her tender way of addressing me. I had picked up on it when I was little more than one and renamed her Amou, even though her real name was Isabella. The affectionate names we had for each other were part of the bond between us, a bond that seemed impossible between me and my mother.

Amou was tall, with hair so vibrantly red, cardinals eyed her jealously. I knew my mother was envious, even though she had beautiful light blond hair herself. She kept her hair short because it required less maintenance, but she had dozens of expensive wigs in a variety of styles.

Still, she was aware of how Amou's hair drew attention. She was always after Amou to cut it, and insisted she keep it tied back tightly. If a strand of it was found anywhere in our house, my mother would hold it between her thumb and forefinger and rage as though rat droppings had been discovered.

I can't recall a time when my mother was nice to Amou. If it wasn't for my father, Amou wouldn't have remained with us long, I'm sure. It couldn't have been because my mother was jealous of how much I cared for Amou and how much she cared for me. My mother insisted Amou remain with us long after I required such attention and care. The only other servant we had was a groundskeeper and driver my father hired. His name was Miles. I didn't think my mother was very fond of him, either, but she had little to do with him.

Amou was a different story. My mother, herself, did become somewhat dependent upon her, over time. Amou, after all, was our cook as well as my nanny, and although we had a separate cleaning woman twice a week, Amou did also look after my mother's things, ironed her clothes, brushed out her wigs, and performed a multitude of small favors. She never argued with my mother or in any way showed any defiance, but her compliance and her willingness to accept the verbal abuse without agreeing or disagreeing only infuriated my mother more. Gradually, as I grew older and more perceptive, I began to understand how Amou undermined and defeated my mother time and time again in her own subtle way.

Amou sat on my bed and held my hand.

"What did I tell you, Willow? I told you to close your eyes and wish away the dreads. It was what my mother taught me. Just think of something nice, something pretty, and push the ugly dreads away," she said.

The scent of her lilac cologne filled my nostrils and soothed my troubled brain. I could feel my body relax, the fear drain out of me. The lightning flashed around us; the thunder clapped, and then, its tail between its legs like some defeated big bad wolf, the storm gradually began to slink away toward some rendezvous with another small frightened child.

Amou remained with me until I closed my eyes again and drifted off, feeling my hand still held softly in hers, hearing her hum one of her Portuguese songs. In the morning all of it seemed like a bad dream, just another in a series of so many floating through our big house, settling in the walls, making each and every room just a little darker.

There was so much darkness in our home that I yearned for brightness and light. I cherished the sound of laughter, and especially held dear any glimmer of joy and pleasure I caught in my father's face when he spoke or gazed at me.

Our house had no reason to be dark. The formal sitting room, the den, the Doctor's office—as my mother insisted I refer to my father—had two large windows right behind his desk, and all of the bedrooms, even Amou's closet of a room, had nice-sized windows. Everywhere there were beautiful views of rolling fields and trees. We had one hundred and fifty acres, and there were wooded paths, two rather large ponds, and a stream that twisted itself over rocks and hills to empty into a larger stream that fed into the Congaree River.

My father and his sister, my aunt Agnes, had inherited the land and the house, but my aunt lived in Charleston and had no interest in the property, so my father paid her for her share. My mother never stopped criticizing him for paying too much. She was not fond of Aunt Agnes, and it was no secret that Aunt Agnes was not fond of her. I could count on the fingers of one hand how often she and her husband and their daughter—my cousin, Margaret Selby—visited our house.

"Your sister simply cannot stand how beautiful I have made this family relic," Mother would tell my father.

The formal rooms, including the dining room, had golden-brown satin curtains with elaborate piping when I was a little girl, but all that, including most of the rooms, had been decorated and redecorated richly three times between my birth and my mother's tragic death in a terrible car accident. She was never satisfied with anything she had done in the house, and went through decorators almost as frequently as she went through brands of makeup. No matter what she did, what she bought, whose advice she cherished at the moment, she would see something someone else had and immediately become critical of her own things. The grass was always greener in someone else's yard.

If the Doctor questioned her sudden dissatisfaction with furniture and drapes and rugs she had relatively recently bought, she would cry and rage at how he was so wrapped up in his work, he had no idea what was in style and what wasn't.

As soon as I was old enough to understand what their arguments were about, if anyone could call them arguments that is, I realized that my father's work and career were a constant source of irritation for my mother. I hesitate to call them arguments, because, like Amou, he put up so little resistance, barely offering any sort of defense or opposition.

"You're not married to me!" my mother would

scream at him. "You're married to that precious clinic of yours, that house of madness you have created. You spend so much time there I should sue you for adultery. How would that look? The perfect psychiatrist, the man who could cure everyone else's messed-up life, can't cure his own?"

For some reason, a reason I wouldn't understand for years and years to come, that particular threat was the only thing that actually dabbed a spot of fear in each of my father's eyes. She wielded it over him like a club, and any resistance, any objection he voiced about something she wanted to buy or spend money on in the house was immediately pulled back and buried under his nod of surrender, his whole body sinking in his chair like the flag of a defeated army.

I didn't know very much about the relationships between men and women yet, and sometimes I wonder if I ever will, but I did believe that, because my mother was so beautiful, my father loved her too deeply and completely to do anything that would displease her too much or too long. He was the most brilliant man I knew, and I knew even when I was only eight that he was a very famous and highly respected man in his field of psychology. There were piles of magazines with his articles in them, and his picture in many. Because the clinic he had created was becoming world-famous, he had been on television often as a guest on talk shows, and was constantly called upon to offer an opinion or a theory about one thing or another, especially in court trials.

I suppose that was why I didn't think it strange that

she insisted I refer to him always as the Doctor when I was speaking about him.

"Don't say my father or my daddy. Say the Doctor," she instructed. After a while, with her watching over my shoulder whenever I spoke, I had trouble thinking of him as anything else but the Doctor.

Despite my age, I sensed that my mother wasn't making me refer to him as the Doctor because she had so much admiration for him. There had to be some other reason. My mother always referred to the Doctor's clinic as either a madhouse or a nuthouse, and I don't know how many times I heard her say what he was doing over there was just high-priced voodoo.

When I was little, he would simply tell me he was going to his hospital. For a long time I thought of it as a place where people went when they had accidents or bad colds, and then one day, when I was little more than seven, I went by his office door and saw him sitting alone, staring out his window. He looked very sad, so I paused and went in to see why.

He didn't hear me for a while, and I was positive I saw him wipe his eyes, just like someone who was crying would.

"What's the matter?" I asked, and he spun around. I thought at first that he was going to be angry I had snuck into his office and watched him, but after a moment, he smiled more warmly than I could ever remember.

"Come here," he beckoned, and I walked around his desk. "Why did you ask me what was the matter?" he wanted to know.

I stood there, gazing down at the floor.

"I thought you were crying," I finally said.

"Well, Willow, you were right. I *was* crying," he revealed.

I couldn't imagine the Doctor crying. Nothing my mother said, no matter how angrily she said it, made him cry. The most dramatic thing I had ever seen him do in response was shake his head with a little expression of disgust on his lips and then walk away.

"Why were you crying?"

"Sometimes, I think about my poor patients and I feel so sorry for them, I can't help it," he told me.

"Because they hurt themselves and they were bleeding?"

"No," he said. "My hospital is different, Willow. My patients are very unhappy or sad people. Sometimes they hurt themselves deliberately and they are taken to the sort of hospital you are thinking of, but after that, they are brought to see me, to see if I can help them feel better about themselves."

"How do you do that?"

He smiled.

"It's hard, but I talk to them a lot. I give them medicines that help and they do things that make them feel better about themselves. They work on art projects or handicrafts, just like you do at school. In fact," he said, brightening even more, "I have something here that I was told to give you a long time ago, but I kept it safe until I thought you were ready for it, old enough for it," he said. "I think you might be old enough now."

"What's that?" I asked, intrigued.

"Just a minute," he said, and went to his office closet, where he took down a box and uncovered it. For a moment he just looked at what was inside as if he was afraid to touch it. Then he lifted it out and showed it to me.

It was a doll, stuffed and sewn with a variety of colorful cloth patches, a real mishmash. Even though the doll's face was made of material similar to my other dolls, it wasn't like any doll I had or any doll I had ever seen in a toy or department store, but it was still very nice.

"It was made especially for you by a very special patient of mine," he told me. "Will you take very good care of it?"

I nodded.

"Okay. Here it is, then. Keep it in a special place in your room."

I took it gingerly into my hands and studied the face. It reminded me of someone, I thought, but I couldn't think of who that was until I had taken it up to my room and stared at it for a long time.

Then it came to me, after I realized the hair color was similar to mine and the face was just like the face in the one picture of me that the Doctor had on his desk, a picture in a silver frame of me when I was about one.

To be sure, when the Doctor was at his clinic and my mother was out shopping, I brought the doll to his office and placed it beside the picture.

The doll face really was my face.

There was no doubt, and this was the biggest mystery I had ever known, and maybe ever would.

# 2

# Rebirth

For me, the darkness really began when I was born again, but not reborn in any good, religious sense. Instead, I was forced to reenter the womb and then be ripped out to discover I was not who I thought I was. My name was not really mine. What was really mine was as insubstantial as smoke, blown away the day I was created, and left to be an unsolved mystery with the title, *Who Am I?*

It had been the Doctor's decision to keep all this from me until he believed I was capable of fully understanding it, and therefore not be deeply emotionally or psychologically harmed by it. The truth had been circling our home like some confused bird, caught up in a harsh wind from time to time and dropping a feather here and there. It tickled my imagination, made me curious and yet confused. I could sense it lingered there on the tip of my mother's tongue, and it was taking all her self-control to keep it locked behind those beautifully shaped lips. She certainly had planted enough hints about our lives, little seeds of ugly truth she wanted to water and sprout.

Finally she couldn't keep it contained any longer, and decided my time had come. I was only eight when she reached this decision, but she was furious at me because she had discovered I had been into her makeup. I had been pretending I was much older and I was going on a date. Actually, I had seen something similar on a television show, where a girl not much older than I was had dressed up in her mother's clothes, put on her mother's makeup and one of her mother's wigs, and then was caught pretending she was her mother speaking to her father. Her parents thought it was cute and everyone had a good time.

However, when my mother caught me at her vanity table, she looked like the blood rising up her neck and into her face would blow off the top of her head. I never saw her swell up as quickly or as tall. The mere sight of her made me cower. How could someone so beautiful, so elegant, someone who drew the admiration of so many other women and so many men look so ugly so quickly?

"WILLOW!" she screamed, and ripped the lipstick out of my hands. She brought it down inches from the edge of my nose. "I put this on my lips!"

It was one thing to be angry I used her things, but another to make me feel as if I was a walking plague, full of disease. I was afraid to cry, to utter a sound, even to breathe. She stared at me a moment, fuming.

"This is ridiculous," she said. "Come with me. Once and for all, you will be made to understand."

She marched me down the stairs and into the living room ahead of her. I felt as if I was being led to a firing squad. If I slowed, she poked me with her forefinger, the long painted nail cutting into my back. Amou, preparing a roast in the kitchen, looked up as we passed by. One glance at my face told her I was utterly terrified, but she would never dare come between me and my mother.

"Sit!" she screamed, pointing to the La-Z-Boy the Doctor loved.

I did so quickly.

"Pay attention!" she ordered. They were nearly always her first words to me, as if she was afraid I could fix my gaze on something else and ignore her completely, just the way the Doctor often did. She wouldn't start until she was satisfied my eyes were directed at her.

"You should know how you came to be living here with us," she began.

*What a strange thing to say,* I thought. When a child is born, she lives with her parents. What is there to know about that?

"You are an adopted child. You understand what that means?" she asked.

I did, but I didn't understand how it could mean me. I did not nod; I did not shake my head. I couldn't move.

"I am not your natural mother. God help me if I

was," she muttered, looking up at the ceiling. She lowered her eyes on me like someone aiming a canon and fired her words. "I am what is more properly known as your adoptive mother. You were born in the Doctor's clinic. That's why I have always wanted you to call him the Doctor instead of Daddy or Papa. He is your adoptive father, understand? He is *not* your daddy or your papa."

She took a deep breath before continuing. To me it seemed as if she were vomiting poison that had been inside her forever and ever.

"Your real mother was one of his patients. You were brought here as part of some cover-up. What a devastating thing it would have been for the world-famous Dr. Claude De Beers to have the world know that one of his patients had been raped in his precious wonderful clinic," she added, wagging her head and speaking in a mocking tone.

She paused again. My eyes were probably as wide and as full of shock as they could be.

"That's right, raped, and by one of the attendants, he says. Maybe she was raped by another patient, I say. Most probably another patient. Both your parents were mentally ill, which, in a way of thinking, helps explain everything."

She stared at me a moment, her head tilted a bit as if she was studying something in my face.

"Do you know what *rape* means?"

I had heard the word often enough on the television news, of course, but I nodded too slowly and with little conviction. Her initial words were still burning through me like hot coals, searing my heart and lungs, making it so difficult to breathe, much less talk.

She wasn't my real mother? The Doctor wasn't my real father? I was to think of them both as my adoptive mother and my adoptive father? My parents were patients? What did she mean by "that explains everything"? It was complicated, but mostly very cold. I felt I was being cut out of their lives. My little bags would be packed and I would be sent on my way to live in some orphanage. Amou would return to Brazil and I would never see her again.

My adoptive mother went on to explain in detail how a rape occurs and how what the rapist deposits in the victim can cause the victim to become pregnant.

"Which is what happened to your real mother. Chances are she didn't even know it was happening to her. Maybe she was one of his catatonic patients. It turns my stomach to think of it," she added with an ugly grimace. She could twist her beautifully shaped lips out of shape and slit her eyes so easily, anyone would think she was composed of rubber.

"Anyway," she continued, bringing her face closer to mine. "I want you to start thinking about how lucky you are we let you live here, how lucky you are *I* let you live here. There is no point in permitting him to lose his wonderful reputation and therefore all of his fancy, wealthy patients, whose families pay the high fees that keep us wealthy, but I don't have to suffer a single instant because of that."

She pulled back, her arms folded under her breasts, her shoulders still hoisted like a hawk's.

Tears burned under my lids, but I was afraid to cry, still afraid to move a muscle.

"Actually, I wanted you to know all this because I want you to understand that you could have inherited insanity of all kinds. I have to be firm with you so we can keep whatever mental disease you might have under control. If you don't, you could end up in the same place. Maybe now you will listen better and behave," she concluded.

She stared at me. "Well, what do you have to say?"

I shook my head slightly. "I don't know," I managed to utter.

"You don't know. I'll tell you what you should say. You should say 'Thank you. Thank you for giving me a nice house to live in, food to fill my stomach, and nice clothing to wear even though I'm not really a De Beers.' That's what you should say. Let me hear it. Go on."

"Thank you," I said through trembling lips.

"Good. Now, before you decide to do anything else that might upset me, you think about all I have told you and what might happen to you if you don't. Is that clearly understood, Willow?"

"Yes," I think I said. I wasn't sure if any sounds came from my lips.

She looked very contented with herself, actually relieved. I watched her walk out. Even after she was gone, I felt her heavy presence over me. It was as if she had left her shadow behind to watch me.

Amou surprised me by coming in a moment later, her face streaking with tears. Apparently, she had followed us and hovered just outside the doorway the whole time.

"Oh, Amou Um, my poor Amou Um," she said, and opened her arms for me.

I felt like a drowning victim, gasping for air, falling into the rescuing arms of my Amou.

"You must not listen to her terrible words, Willow. You must not," she said, and repeated it like a prayer. "No one is worthless who is born. God makes children. You have no disease in you, nothing bad in you. Okay?"

I nodded, but as one too stunned to really appreciate what she was being told or what she was agreeing to by nodding. Amou held me and rocked with me. My little heart pounded, and then, afterward, when she went back to her dinner preparations, I ran off behind the house and hid myself behind the biggest oak tree. I remained out there for hours and hours. When Amou called for me, I did not answer, nor did I go back. I crouched deeper into the shadows, even though it was so hard to ignore her pleas.

I was more comfortable out here, bathed in the darkness. I didn't fully understand everything my adoptive mother had told me, but it was enough to make me feel so empty. It was as if my body had lost all of its substance, and if I didn't cling to something, I might get caught up in the wind and carried off.

The Doctor was away on a speaking engagement. He was often on those, and this one had taken him clear across the country to California. He was gone nearly three whole days, and during that time I continued to mope and hide from my adoptive mother's suspicious and critical eyes as much as I could. I spent most of my time wandering alone outside the house. When it was time for dinner and I knew my adoptive mother would be there at the table with me, I actually felt myself trembling. I had little appetite, too.

Before the Doctor returned, I developed a fever and Amou kept me in bed, bringing me my meals. My adoptive mother didn't think I was really sick, and Amou had to show her the thermometer. She drove her away by suggesting I might be coming down with something contagious. As it turned out, I never developed a cold or a cough, and as quickly as my fever had come, it was gone.

When the Doctor returned, he asked for me, and Amou told him what had happened. My adoptive mother was at a charity event. He came right to my room, which was not something he had often done. I thought he might be angry at me.

He never yelled at me, but whenever he spoke to me with my adoptive mother present, he always spoke firmly, sounding more like a schoolteacher than a father, adoptive or otherwise. With Amou at his side this time, he spoke much more softly, even lovingly.

He knelt down and took my hands.

"I'm sorry you heard that the way you did, Willow," he began.

"I'm adopted," I said, hoping he would deny it, hoping he would tell me my mother was simply angry again and was saying something that wasn't really true, but he just nodded.

"Yes, you are adopted, Willow, but that doesn't

mean you are less to me. You are our daughter and this is your home. This room is still your room and all your dolls and toys are still yours. This is not any less your home than it was before you were told these things."

I wanted to ask him about the word *rape*. I wanted to ask him if I was going to be a patient in his clinic, too, someday, but I didn't.

"I was planning on telling you everything someday, Willow, but I was hoping to wait until you were somewhat older, so you could understand everything easier," he explained. "I want you to know that nothing will change. Nothing is any different. You are Willow De Beers and you will always be, until you get married, that is," he added with a smile. "Although many women keep their maiden names these days," he said, more to Amou than to me. "Come, get out of bed, wash your face, and put on something nice. Then come on downstairs," he said, standing. "It's almost time for dinner, and then afterward, you and I can read your schoolbook together."

It was one of the few things he did with me on a regular basis.

While I was getting dressed, my mother returned, and I heard them talking. The Doctor didn't raise his voice, but he was getting her more and more upset. I could tell by the shrill sound of her replies and how she was getting louder and louder.

"I did what you should have done a long time ago," she concluded. "You're an expensive psychiatrist, Claude, but you don't seem to know how to handle your own situations at home, and I warned you at the start that I wouldn't put up with anything that made me unhappy."

He didn't respond apparently, because I didn't hear him. I heard doors close and his footsteps in the hallway.

Later, at dinner, my adoptive mother—as I could not help but think of her now—acted as if nothing terrible had been said and told. She chatted on about her social plans, something new she wanted to buy for the house, and a vacation she was thinking they should take. It was as if I wasn't even there, as if her earlier words had made me invisible. I felt the Doctor's eyes on me from time to time, but other than that, and Amou's talking to me, I imagined myself drifting away, like an astronaut whose lifeline in space had been cut. I was floating into the darkness, helplessly.

At school I couldn't help wondering if I suddenly appeared different to my friends and my teachers. Did some of them always know the truth anyway? Was it something in my school records? There was one other adopted child in my classes, a boy named Scott Lawrence. For some reason his status as an adopted child was never kept secret. Of course, my adoptive mother had made it perfectly clear that I was a major embarrassment for the Doctor and his clinic, and so I had to be hush-hush. My very existence was a whisper.

Now that I had been so bluntly told the truth and left with the idea that madness could sprout in my face anytime, anywhere, I was sure anyone and everyone who looked at me instantly realized what I was.

At night I would lie awake and wonder what my

real mother's name was and, of course, what she looked like. I would stare at myself in the mirror and study my eyes to see if there was someone crazy just waiting to pop out of me. And I would have terrible new nightmares about my birth.

I knew what someone in a catatonic state was like because I had wandered into the Doctor's office from time to time and looked at some of his textbooks. I saw a picture of a woman who was catatonic. She looked like she was imprisoned in her own body. There were tubes connected to her, which was how she got food. When I asked the Doctor about it, he said sometimes people shut themselves up in their own bodies to escape from unpleasant things. They don't see or hear or even feel anything anymore.

A baby made in such a woman would grow like a plant, I thought. Her mother would not even realize she was in her until it was time for her to come out. The mother might have to be cut open and the baby taken out. Afterward, the sewed up mother wouldn't even know a baby had been there. Was that the way it had been for my real mother?

Maybe she didn't know I even existed, that a part of her was alive. She didn't name me or ever feed me— she probably didn't so much as look at me and smile. I was just something that was, something without any history. My adoptive mother was right, I supposed. I should be very grateful for what she and the Doctor were giving me. They were giving me a name and a home.

I couldn't help but be more curious about Scott

Lawrence now. What image did he have of himself? Did he wonder about his real parents, too? Did he especially wonder whether or not he had any brothers or sisters? Could I have any? Was my mother married before she went to the clinic and could she have had other children before she became mentally ill?

I couldn't really imagine Scott Lawrence being bothered by anything like this. Of all the boys in my class, he was one of the most outgoing, if not *the* most outgoing. There was nothing even to suggest he had any sort of inferiority complex. In fact, some of the boys thought he verged on the border of being a bully. He was hyper in class and loved to pull practical jokes on the girls, especially shy ones like me. Getting him or any of the boys in my fifth-grade class to be serious for a few minutes was as hard as keeping a fish out of water calm.

Nevertheless, one day shortly after my terrible confrontation with my adoptive mother, I decided to chance it. We had a forty-five-minute lunch hour, but most everyone gobbled down his or her food in less than fifteen minutes and then spent the rest of the lunch hour in the shady area just outside the cafeteria. Our teachers who were on lunch duty monitored it as well as the lunchroom. We were not permitted to leave the designated section of the school grounds. Outside, students could play radios or CD players if they did so at a decent volume. Ordinarily, the boys stayed apart from the girls. We would laugh at the way some of them showed off, their fooling around and roughhousing occasionally breaking out into a more serious fight. Scott certainly had more than his share of those and, in fact, was on probation.

I could see that some of his friends were trying to encourage him to do something outrageous. They loved seeing someone else get into trouble. Their catcalls and challenges were making Scott's cheeks crimson. Mr. Anderson eyed him suspiciously, looking as if he was just waiting to pounce. I wandered close to Scott and said, "Don't let them get you in trouble."

He turned, his blond eyebrows lifted with surprise. Everyone thought he resembled the illustration of Huckleberry Finn that was on the cover of the copy in our library. He had hair that jetted up and out and was kept short. He had the same impish eyes, with a face spotted with freckles, and lips the color of orange sherbet. In an instant he could look sweet and innocent, but as soon as the teacher's eyes shifted away, he could turn into an imp with eyes full of mischief.

"If they were really your friends, they wouldn't be doing that," I added.

"I know," he said. "They don't bother me."

"Good," I muttered, and looked away.

"How come you're not hangin' out with Madonna and her friends?" he asked me, referring to Selma Thursten, whose parents had permitted her to put a ring in her navel. She already had the suggestion of an oncoming bosom and wore tight pants with blouses that showed some midriff, especially after she acquired the ring. Scott often teased her by threatening to stick his pinky finger through it and rip it away. Anyone could see she enjoyed being teased and screaming at him whenever he did it in our halls and school classrooms.

I shrugged. "I don't think she's anyone special," I told him.

He liked that. "She isn't. You're more special than she is," he added, surprising me.

"I am?"

"Sure," he said. He picked up a rock and threw it dangerously close to Mr. Anderson, who didn't see it.

"Why do you do things like that?" I asked him.

"Do what?"

"Take such chances of getting into more trouble?"

"Nothing better to do," he quipped, but then looked quickly to see how I reacted. I smirked. "I don't know," he added, and looked a little remorseful. Then, as if he felt he was showing some sign of weakness, he added, "Why do you care if I get in trouble or not? I'm not one of your precious friends, am I?"

"I don't have any precious friends." I hesitated and then, after a deep breath, said, "I found out something terrible about myself." Then I thought *terrible* might not be the right word to use, especially with him. "Secret, I mean."

"What's that?"

"If I tell you, will you swear you will keep it a secret?"

"No," he said.

I looked away.

"All right. I swear, but it better be good, real good." Then he thought again and asked, "Why are you telling me anyway?"

I looked at him, my eyes small, but dark and firm enough to impress him.

"Because you're the only one I know who might understand," I said.

His curiosity whetted, he softened his posture and looked very serious and interested.

"Why?"

"Because you're adopted."

"So?"

"I'm adopted, too. That's what I found out," I told him.

His first reaction was to look skeptical and even threaten to laugh out loud, but the expression on my face stopped him and brought him closer to me.

"True?"

"Yes," I said.

Something in his face changed dramatically. It was like a smile coming up from under the mask he usually wore. He glanced at the others and then looked at me.

"None of your precious friends knows?"

I shook my head.

"Big deal," he said after another moment, and then he turned and charged at one of his friends, deliberately knocking him into Mindy Hasbrouck, which started enough of a commotion to make Mr. Anderson chase everyone back into the cafeteria.

I thought that was the end of it, and decided to put my great secret back into the safe locked behind my heart, but Scott surprised me that day by following the van that took me and four other students home after school. He rode behind us on his bike. No one else noticed him but me. When I got out to walk up my driveway, I waited for him to catch up. He bounced over pavement and skidded to a stop inches from me.

"You gotta go right home?" he asked.

I looked at the front of the house. Amou usually waited for me after school. The Doctor was at his clinic and my adoptive mother was either out with friends shopping or attending some charity event.

"No," I said.

"Good. Get on," he ordered, pounding his seat.

Courageously, I did so.

"Hold on," he told me, and shot away. There was a steep hill just down from our property and he didn't slow much to descend. I screamed and closed my eyes, and he laughed.

"Make way!" he shouted. "Make way for the Adopted."

Not only wasn't it a secret to him, he was eager to rub it in the face of Fate.

No adoptive mother would bring him to tears. Was it all a facade, an act to serve as a suit of armor? *Even if it is,* I thought, *I want to be like him.* Before our bike ride ended, I was screaming with him:

"Make way for the Adopted!"

# 3

# Love Is in the Heart, Not the Blood

It wasn't until I went to Scott's home one weekend afternoon that I understood what gave him his self-confidence and strength. His adoptive father was a plumber and his adoptive mother, once a secretary, was now doing only freelance work, but not because she couldn't find a full-time job. Before Scott invited me to his home, he revealed that his mother (he never referred to her or his father as adoptive) was suffering from something called lupus. It was a debilitating illness, and from what he understood and what his father had told him, his mother was getting worse. She had been sick for nearly eight years.

"Sometimes she has a lot of pain," he explained to me. "And she doesn't like to see people, but she's okay right now and she told me you could come over."

Despite her illness, Scott's mother was a very pleasant woman. She was sickly thin, I thought, but she had a nice smile with soft blue eyes. She was a dark brunette, and almost as tall as Amou. I could see that it was painful for her to move about the house, but she wouldn't let it stop her from making Scott and me some homemade chocolate chip cookies. What surprised me the most that first day I met her was that Scott had told her my secret.

The moment she revealed that, I turned sharply and glared angrily at Scott. His mother saw how upset I was.

"Scott doesn't keep secrets from me, Willow. We love each other too much to ever hide things from each other or lie to each other," she explained.

I turned back to her and saw she was very sincere. *Love each other too much?* I wondered. But . . .

"I even know how often he gets himself in trouble at school, don't I, Scott?" she asked, her eyes narrow, threatening.

He nodded and then smiled.

"However, he has recently promised me he won't be getting into trouble any longer, right, Scott?"

"A-huh," Scott said.

"We know the value of a promise in this house, too, don't we, Scott?"

He nodded again and then raised his eyes to see how I was reacting to this little cross-examination his mother was holding.

His mother settled back on the settee, pulling the light blanket she had at her knees up a bit, and turned her attention more to me.

"Scott says you just recently learned about yourself. Is that true, Willow?"

"Yes, ma'am," I said.

"It's not an easy thing to live with. I know. Everyone treats it differently, I suppose, and I suppose no one should know better about that than a man like your father, but we thought it was better for Scott to know everything as soon as we thought he would understand, because we wanted him to know without a doubt that we couldn't love him any more than we already did.

"Besides," she continued, smiling at Scott, "I had him in my arms moments after he was born, anyway. I gave him his first bottle and I changed his first diaper."

She stopped smiling and turned back to me.

"When other people find out about you, some of them are going to look at you differently. That's because they won't know what to expect. Too often children get measured in terms of their parents. If someone's father is a good athlete, they expect his son to be, or if a girl's mother has a nice singing voice, they expect she'll have one, too.

"But you're a bit of a mystery, and that sometimes makes other people uncomfortable. Scott and I and his father have talked about these things many times, haven't we, Scott?"

"Yes," he said.

"We want him to be comfortable with himself. I suppose your father will be doing something similar with you, if he hasn't already, and your mother," she added.

I wanted to tell her, *no, my mother would never do*

*anything like that,* but I was ashamed of it, especially there and then in the glow of the love she and Scott obviously shared. I don't think I ever felt as poor as I did that moment. I had a bigger home and we had so many more expensive things in it, but Scott Lawrence was far wealthier than I was, I thought.

"Why don't you show Willow your and your father's electric trains," his mother said, closing her eyes a bit and sinking in the settee. "I need a little rest, honey."

"Yeah," Scott said. "C'mon."

He grabbed my hand and tugged me roughly off the chair to lead me through the house. In a room down from the kitchen, Scott and his father had installed one of the most elaborate and wonderful sets of electric trains I had ever seen. The trains ran through a miniature city with tiny people, cars, buses, even school buses. There was so much to see.

Scott went to the controls and put on a train engineer's cap.

"Here we go," he declared, and started the engine that pulled boxcars and flat cars and passenger cars with people in the little windows. He began a second train that ran under and around the first. They even made sounds and sent little puffs of smoke up in the air. Some of the storefronts had lights that flickered on.

"How long did it take to make this?" I asked.

"Me and Dad been workin' on it for years and years," he said proudly. "You want to work this?" he offered, showing me the controls. "Go on, try it."

I did, and while I did, he went to a partially constructed new building, a lumberyard company, and started to work on the tiny sticks.

"I told Dad I'd finish this one before he got home from work today," he said.

What impressed me most about the tiny toy city and the trains was the obvious love and care that had gone into it, that was still going into it. *How many, many hours must Scott and his father have spent here together,* I thought. How jealous it made me.

Scott's mother was very sick, but there was so much less darkness in this house than there was in mine. *No wonder he couldn't care less about his being an adopted child,* I thought. There were probably dozens of children in our class who were naturally born to their parents and did not share half as much of their love and life.

I visited Scott's house often after that. I wanted to invite him to mine, but my adopted mother did not like the idea of my having friends over. It would be years before she relented, and only after the Doctor assured her they wouldn't be tracking in any dirt or touching any of her expensive things. When I did have friends over, I always thought of areas of the house as having invisible tape roping them off. We could look into the rooms, but not set foot in them. I was sure my friends never felt half as comfortable as I did at Scott's or at their houses, and I understood why coming to my house was not something they were eager to do.

About a year after I had met Scott's mother, she died. I knew she had been taken to the hospital. During those days and weeks, he became a very withdrawn person, barely saying anything to anyone but me. Our teachers knew of the difficulties he and his father were facing, and they didn't call upon him or pressure him in class.

The day I heard his mother had died, I rode my bike to his house. Some of his father's and his mother's relatives had already arrived and were setting up food and preparing for the funeral. Scott had closed himself in his room. His father was happy I had come and hoped I would be able to bring him out. I didn't know what I was going to say to him. The only death in our family I knew about was the Doctor's uncle, his father's brother, and I had seen him only once. He was in his late eighties when he died, and there wasn't much if any grief in anyone's face at the funeral, especially not my adoptive mother's face.

This was far different, of course. I knocked on his door and waited after I called to him, but he didn't respond. I was undecided about what to do. Should I continue to knock or should I try the door to see if it was unlocked?

"I just want to tell you how sorry I am, Scott," I said to the closed door.

I was about to turn and walk away when it opened. It seemed to open by itself, because he wasn't standing there. I walked in and saw he had gone back to his bed, where he was sprawled on his back, looking up at the ceiling. His eyes were red, but there were no tears.

"Are you all right?" I asked him.

"No," he said.

"Your father is worried about you," I told him.

He raised his head and glared furiously at me.

"He told me he wasn't going to let her die. He told me. He promised!" he cried.

"I'm sure he did all he could do," I said softly.

"It wasn't enough. He shouldn't have promised."

"He probably didn't want you to worry," I offered.

Scott glared back at me as if I was part of some horrible betrayal.

"We don't lie to each other in this house, remember?"

"I don't think it was meant to be a lie," I said.

"Well, it was!" he shouted. "It was!"

I looked down. His face was burning with so much fury, it was painful to look at him, and even frightening.

"I wasn't supposed to have a mother," he declared. "She shouldn't have adopted me. I was supposed to be an orphan. My father will die, too," he concluded.

I started to shake my head.

"It's true. It's the same for you," he snapped. "You'll see. We're not supposed to have a family. Ask your father. Ask your father to send you back to your real mother and see what he says. He'll tell you she's either dead or she doesn't want you."

I bit down on my lower lip. He was bringing tears to my eyes. His words were like little knives scratching and cutting into my heart.

I started to shake my head and he jumped up, seized my hand, and pulled me out of his room.

"Come on," he said, leading me down the stairs.

Relatives started toward him, but he ignored them all and charged along the hallway. I followed behind, confused, but afraid to stop. He led me past the kitchen and down to the train room, where he threw the door open and then stepped back. I looked at him, confused, and then I looked through the doorway and my heart stopped.

The little city was wrecked, the houses smashed and thrown about. Railroad cars were crushed as well. It was as if a bomb had fallen on the whole thing.

Finally tears began to stream down my cheeks.

"Why?" I managed to utter.

"Because this was a lie, too!" he screamed. He was crying now. "It's fake. Everything is fake!"

He stood there for a moment, his shoulders shaking, and then he turned and ran to the back door of the house and out. The door slammed shut behind him. For a few moments, I couldn't move. I was shaking so badly.

"He'll be all right," I heard, and turned to see his father. "It will take time, but he will be all right," he said, smiling, his eyes as red as Scott's. "I'll go after him. Thanks for coming to see him," he told me, touched my shoulder, and then walked slowly to the back door.

I sobbed most of my way home. When I arrived, I went directly to the rear of the house, where we had benches. There were walkways through the gardens and bushes that led to the woods. The Doctor loved to go for long walks. Usually, he did so alone, but on occasion, he took me with him. He wouldn't walk as long or as far then. We talked about things and he asked me lots of questions.

I didn't know he was home and had gone for a walk this afternoon, so I was surprised when he suddenly appeared, returning from the woods and fields.

"Willow," he said, approaching and smiling at me. "I asked Isabella where you were and she said you had gone for a bike ride to see your friend Scott. Everything all right?" he asked, wondering why I was back so soon, I suppose.

"No. His mother died," I said angrily.

"Oh. Oh, I'm sorry to hear that. You did tell me she was a very sick woman."

"Why didn't the doctors help her?" I demanded.

Even though I understood that he was involved solely with the illness of the mind, I did not separate him from the world of medicine and doctors I knew. They were all part of the same grand machine that was supposed to make us well again and repair our injuries. They were his people, and they had failed.

He sat beside me. "You know there are many illnesses that we can't yet cure, don't you, Willow?"

"Yes," I reluctantly replied.

"Should you be angry at the doctors who tried to help her then?"

I didn't want him to be right, but he was. "No."

"That's all right, though. I understand how you feel. We often blame the wrong people for things, but maybe it's because we put so much hope and faith in them."

That struck a familiar note.

"Scott's mad at his father. He said he promised his mother wouldn't die."

"Oh, I see. Well, why do you think his father did that?"

"So he wouldn't worry."

"So his father didn't do it to hurt him then, did he?"

"No. But he shouldn't have promised," I added on Scott's behalf. "Lies weren't supposed to happen in his house."

"No, they shouldn't happen in anyone's house."

He was quiet a moment, and I wondered if, finally, the Doctor had no answers.

"I wouldn't want to ever tell you to lie," he continued. "But sometimes it's all right to give people some hope. It helps keep them healthy and productive. How would Scott have been if his father had told him a long time ago that his mother was going to die soon?"

"Bad," I admitted.

"And would he be able to go to school and enjoy his friends and even sleep well at night?"

"No."

"So, did his father do a bad thing to him?"

"No," I said.

"Maybe afterward, when a little time passes, you can help Scott see that, too. Then you'll be a very good friend to him, Willow."

I nodded.

*The Doctor does have all the answers,* I thought.

He patted me on the knee and rose.

"Looks like we might get some rain tonight," he said, looking out over the trees. "Flowers need it."

Sometimes I thought he was speaking to me, but he really wasn't. I was just there. He would look at me, but I felt he was looking past me, looking at someone else who was in his eyes. It gave me a funny feeling.

"Well, I've got some work to do," he concluded and went inside.

I wanted to go to Scott's mother's funeral, but my mother wouldn't take me and the Doctor had to be at his clinic. I thought about getting on my bike and riding all the way; however, I knew it was too far and it would take me too long. I did go to his house afterward and sat with him. There were so many people there, friends of his father's from work, more relatives. He and I didn't talk that much.

He was different when he returned to school. No longer as outgoing, he lost his impish quality, and if he got into any arguments or fights, they were far more vicious and brutal. He was in trouble more often.

Then, one day, he didn't come to school. He didn't come the next day, either. On the third day I rode to his house and saw a sign on the lawn advertising that it was for sale. The windows were dark and his father's pickup truck was not in the driveway. I went up to the front door and pushed the buzzer, but no one answered. When I looked in the window, I saw the furniture was gone.

I remember I snapped back as if I had burned my forehead on the glass.

Later, I found out his father had gotten another job through one of their relatives who lived in Virginia. I was very sad over it, but I didn't have anyone to talk to about it. The Doctor was particularly busy at the time. I overheard that he had nearly a half dozen new patients admitted. Some days he didn't come home until after dinner. My adoptive mother complained about it for a while and then, as if something in her head snapped, she stopped. In fact, I sensed that she no longer cared if he was home or not.

She was angry about my being unhappy, though, and did complain to him again and again about my moods.

"I know enough about manic-depression, thanks to you, to know she's a prime candidate, Claude. Don't think I'm going to tolerate any of that in this house," she warned.

He assured her I was just experiencing what all young girls experience as they move into adolescence.

"I never acted like that," she told him.

He didn't answer, which was an answer she missed.

I spent most of my time trying to avoid her, and then doing my best to put on an act she would accept. *How different our home is from Scott's,* I remember thinking. Here, truth is rare; lies are the coin we use to buy peace and toleration of each other.

Sometimes it felt as if the floor were trembling beneath my feet. The whole structure would come down around us in a grand collapse, and the Doctor could do nothing to stop it. I imagined the seams pulling apart, the very walls severing.

I was sixteen by then, and we were all living separate lives. As a kind of negotiated settlement between my adoptive mother and the Doctor, I was permitted to refer to her as 'Mother' only when we were out or amongst people, so that there could be at least the semblance of a normal home life. In the house, however, she began to insist I call her Alberta.

"Since I'm not your mother," she told me, "it makes more sense."

It was just another in a series of sour balls for me to swallow.

One day I heard a little girl tell her mother she had to go to the bathroom. I was in the lobby of the movie theater with two of my friends from school. Her mother made a pained expression and groaned so loudly, people stopped talking around her.

"What?" she demanded, tugging the little girl's arm.

"A BM," she replied, and the mother went charging off to the ladies' room.

I couldn't help recalling so many times when my adoptive mother treated me that insensitively, and suddenly it occurred to me.

I wouldn't think of her or refer to her as my adoptive mother anymore.

I would call her my AM.

Just never to her face. . . .

"Why are you smiling?" one of my girlfriends asked.

"Am I smiling? I must be happy," I replied.

The two of them shook their heads and laughed at my glee. It was not important why one of us was happy, actually. The mood was catching. All giggles, we hurried into the theater, taking joy in our youth without ever really appreciating how precious and how short-lived it was.

# 4

# Heartbreak and Fate

Perhaps no day in my life was as dark and as sad for me as the day Amou told me she was going to leave. She told me before she told my AM or even the Doctor. Somehow, I never thought of her as leaving our home. Of course, I knew she and her older sister Marisa had left their family behind in Brazil. Two years before, Marisa had returned to Brazil. I suspected from reading between the lines that the Doctor had prevented Amou from going by raising her salary significantly and by paying for her vacation trip to Rio. I didn't really understand why he was so determined to keep her in our family. I assumed it was because of the many things she was still doing for my AM.

I was at my desk, doing my homework, when she came to my room. Even though I could sense when she was near, I suspected she had been standing in my doorway watching me for a good half minute or so before bringing herself to my attention.

"What, Amou?" I asked, smiling at her.

"I am always surprised at how grown-up you have become," she said, "how beautiful you are. *Muito lindo.*"

My face flushed crimson and I laughed.

Once, when I was about fourteen, my AM had come into my room, stood there looking at me, shaking her head, and then said, "Your real mother must have been a chunky woman with a double chin. Probably with oversized, sagging breasts and a waist you could tie an ocean liner to when it was in port. She was probably short and squatty with ballooned cheeks and tiny eyes. Medicine, especially the medicine they give mentally ill people, can do that to a person, you know, and then their offspring inherit it."

I had run to Amou immediately after and told her. Now I reminded her of that.

"Remember? She said I would be forever bloat-faced."

Amou waved at the air as if she were waving away annoying flies and came into my room. For a moment she just stood there, looking at everything, just the way someone would who wanted to commit it all to memory forever. It started a small alarm in my heart that confused me.

"What's wrong, Amou?" I asked.

She smiled and sat on my bed. I turned my chair around.

"My sister is a lonely woman now that both our

parents are gone," she began, "and there is something in my heart that cries not only for her, but for my youth. It is time for me to go home, Amou Um."

"Go home?"

In my mind, this had always been Amou's home. How could she think of anywhere else as her home?

"Back to my roots, my people, my uncles and aunts and cousins. I have so many nieces and nephews, I can't remember all their names," she added.

"Oh," I said. It was like all my insides were crumbling.

"You must not be upset, Willow. You really are a grown woman now. You do not need someone like me trailing after you all the time. Soon, you will be serious with some young man, I'm sure, and you would forget me, anyway."

"I could never forget you, Amou. Don't say such a terrible thing!" I cried.

She laughed. "When a girl becomes a woman, she forgets a lot more than she ever thought she would, but that's not something bad. It is what should be. It's only natural. Do not be upset at yourself for that," she insisted.

"When are you going?"

"In a week. Dr. De Beers doesn't know exactly, but he has been anticipating it for some time, I'm sure," she said. "Of course, I will miss him very much, too."

I could feel the tears flowing over my lids and starting down my cheeks.

"I'll never see you again," I moaned.

"Of course you will see me again. I will come back

often, and maybe someday, when you are able, you will travel to Brazil and I will be able to show you my beautiful country."

My throat closed. I turned away.

"I'll hate living here without you," I threatened. "I'll run away."

I turned back to her.

"Maybe I'll run away to Brazil."

"The Doctor would be very upset, Willow. You don't want to hurt him so much, do you?"

"He's never here. He hardly sees me these days. I almost agree with my AM about it," I said, dabbing my eyes with a tissue. "He's married to the clinic. It's his whole life."

"No," she insisted. "You are his whole life."

"Oh, sure," I said.

"Maybe no one should be anyone's whole life," she added, far more thoughtful and philosophical than I had ever seen her. "It's good to be a little selfish. So you can survive," she added. "You look at me like you don't understand, but I'm sure, some day, you will," she said, smiling.

"Oh, Amou."

I rose and threw my arms around her. We held each other for a long moment, rocking just the way I used to when I was very little and afraid or had just been hurt. Then she let go of me and I let go of her.

She stood up, and I saw she had tears welling in her eyes, too.

"You have been my *filha*," she said, which was Portuguese for "daughter."

"And you have been my *mae*," I told her, which was Portuguese for "mother."

How well those words fit the both of us.

I cried myself to sleep that night. The next day I could easily tell she had informed both my AM and the Doctor. My AM was even more nasty and sarcastic than ever, which I didn't think possible.

"Normal people give their employers a month's notice," she said at breakfast when Amou brought in the coffee. It was as if she had been holding the sentence on her lips all night.

Amou poured her and the Doctor their coffee without speaking.

"To be fair," the Doctor said after a moment, "I would have to admit Isabella has been saying she intended on leaving very soon for some time now."

He smiled at Amou. "None of us wanted to believe it, Isabella, but we all understand."

"*I* don't understand," my AM snapped. "How can you want to return to the Third World and live in squalor when you can enjoy living in upper-class America?"

"My family does not live in squalor, Mrs. De Beers."

"Umph," my AM muttered.

"I wouldn't exactly call Brazil Third World, Alberta," the Doctor said softly.

"Right. It's paradise on earth."

"Paradise is wherever you are most happy," Amou said.

Since she rarely, if ever, even approached or hinted

at contradicting my AM, her remark raised all our eyebrows at once.

"Oh, and you're not happy here, making a queen's salary for maid's work?"

"I have come to an end here, Mrs. De Beers. You will find someone else very quickly, I'm sure."

"I'm sure, too. Especially if we offer half of what we give you."

Amou sewed her mouth closed and finished serving our breakfast. I said nothing. The Doctor returned to his magazine and my AM sat smoldering. I imagined the smoke pouring out of her ears.

It was a very hard week for me. In school, I would suddenly break out in tears. My friends were confused. I never wanted anyone to know just how close I was to Amou. None of them would understand how I could be so emotionally tied to a house servant and care more about her than I did my mother.

The day Amou left, I went with her to the airport. The Doctor drove her. My AM didn't so much as say goodbye. I heard her threaten the Doctor, however, should he go and give "that woman" any sort of bonus.

"You should charge back what it will cost us to have the house managed until we find a decent replacement," she told him.

I smiled to myself about that when I saw the Doctor hand Amou an envelope at the airport. He said goodbye to her and then went out to the car to wait for me. I stayed with her until they called for her plane to be boarded.

"You must not think of this as a goodbye," she told me. "It's just a little space between us that we will close often, Amou Um."

"I know," I said.

"I can give you no more than you can give to yourself now. You will be a wonderful woman, and I know, when your time comes, you will be a wonderful mother and a wonderful wife. Take care of Dr. De Beers," she concluded.

I thought it was a strange thing for her to tell me to do. How could I ever be the one to take care of the Doctor? He was the one who took care of everyone else.

"He needs your understanding," she added.

She hugged and kissed me and then she started for the gate door. I waited until she turned, waved, and threw me a kiss. Moments later she was gone.

When I got back into our car, the Doctor reached across to squeeze my hand gently.

"I know you're sad, Willow, but Isabella is going home to her family, to people she loves and who love her and who miss her deeply. Don't you think you should be happy for Isabella?"

"Yes," I said in a small, reluctant voice.

"It's not like you will never see her again, is it?"

"No."

"You know you have a lot to do during the next two years. You will be graduating high school and thinking about a college education. You will be thinking about what you want to do with yourself. Have you given it any consideration?"

"Yes."

"What ideas do you have?"

"I think I want to go into psychology, too," I said. "I think I want to help people."

"That's very nice, Willow. I think you could be very successful at that. If you ever have any questions you want answered, please come to me, okay?"

"Yes," I said.

"I'm already very proud of your accomplishments at school," he said.

"When did you know what you wanted to be?" I asked him.

"Oh, not until my first year of college, really. For a while I thought I might go into teaching, and then I thought I would like to do something about the so-called unteachable, those troubled souls who are too often forgotten or discarded. Bringing someone back from that is like . . ."

"What?"

"Bringing someone back from the dead," he replied. He smiled. "We don't have that sort of success all that often, but when we do, it makes you feel it's all been worth it. I know I should be spending more time with you, but that's been what's kept me from doing it. Maybe now, I will," he suddenly decided. "I will."

"I'd like that," I said.

He nodded and we drove on in silence, my eyes and my ears filled with Amou's last moments with me.

I had no idea what his were filled with, but when I looked at him, he seemed just as sad, if not sadder than I was.

And I wondered why, what it could be that would have such an effect on him.

It wasn't going to be for a while yet before I would find out, but when I did, I fully understood every dark moment I had ever caught him having.

Postcards from Brazil began arriving within two weeks of Amou's departure. I wrote her long letters, sometimes spending more time on them than I did on my homework. I wanted to get every little detail of our lives in the letters. I knew she would enjoy hearing about the three new maids my AM hired and fired within weeks of each other. If one cooked well, she didn't clean well; if she cleaned well, she couldn't cook; and if she could do both well, she had no idea how to brush out a wig.

"I guess Isabella was worth what we paid her after all," the Doctor said one night.

Finally my AM had no reply. Her silence was her admittance of being wrong. What she did instead was turn to me and say, "You should be doing more around here until we find someone suitable. Apparently, you're smart enough to be on the honor roll at school all the time. Nothing here should be a challenge."

It was almost a compliment. The Doctor looked at me, his eyes twinkling with amusement.

"I'll do whatever I can to help, Alberta."

She said nothing, but when we were between maids, I prepared one of Amou's favorite dishes: peixe oporto, which was baked white fish with a port wine sauce. I had stood beside her and watched and helped her do it many times. She always welcomed me in the kitchen, teaching me all sorts of little culinary secrets. I knew my AM loved this dish. When I brought it out and she and the Doctor began to eat it, I could see the pleasure and surprise in both their faces, especially hers.

"Brains, looks, and this, too," the Doctor said.

It wasn't that often that he gave me such compliments in front of my AM. I blushed with pride, and I saw her turn to me and look at me with an expression I had not seen before. It was as if she finally had taken a good look at me and at who I was. I could almost hear something click in her head.

I did some more cooking for us after that, but a week later my AM did find a cook and a maid who satisfied her. She was in her late fifties. Her name was Molly Williams, and she appeared to have the sort of personality my AM appreciated: a private person who was efficient and wasted few words. At times I thought she was robotic, but by now, as Amou predicted, my interests were developing in things outside our home. I participated in more school activities, was in a school play, and was even on the girls' field hockey team. The Doctor attended some of the games, and to my surprise, my AM accompanied him to the school play. I didn't have that big of a role, but it was enough for me to make an impression.

Whatever had clicked in my AM's mind that night I made my first dinner had an effect afterward on the way she behaved toward me. It began in little ways. She would make a comment about my hair and then, to my surprise this time, suggest some product she was using that would improve my texture, bring out the color, and keep it softer. She began to do the same with makeup, and especially her miraculous skin creams and facial treatments. She even invited me to join her at her spa one weekend. I began to have the feeling I had become a project for her. On a few occasions I heard her brag about how much of an improvement in my appearance she had made.

The Doctor seemed amused by all this, but also quite happy. Our once quite estranged little family began to take on the semblance of a unit. My AM was always quite involved in a variety of charity functions and always as a cosponsor or co-chair, always someone important. She surprised me again by inviting me to volunteer to help with some of these events.

Perhaps time and the inevitability of my continuing existence in her life finally had a positive influence on her. I did not know the reason, but I was grateful for the little truces between us. This didn't make a significantly dramatic change in her personality. She was still hard and cold more often than not, and her suggestions for my improvements always came on the heels of some nasty remark.

Nor did any of this make a significant dent in the wall I sensed had grown in height and thickness between her and the Doctor. His work at the clinic still dominated his day and his life, and she never eased up on her complaints about it. To be sure, there were isolated moments when they seemed to be softer toward each other. I sensed the Doctor still liked to dress up and be seen with her. She had, whether it be because

of her constant pampering of herself or not, an endur-
ing beauty and made a striking figure, especially when
she wore one of her expensive gowns.

Despite the way she often belittled and disparaged
the Doctor's profession, she was an orthodox believer
in the theory that stress degenerated and eventually
killed someone. Whenever something made her angry,
she would go right to one of her pampering processes—
whether it be a facial, a massage, a mud bath, a herbal
bath, whatever—to counter the negative effects. I had
seen her do that time and time again when I was little
and she was barking at me for one thing or another.

Perhaps that belief in the importance of contentment and its significant influence on the aging process
had the most to do with the changes that I saw in her
behavior toward me and toward the Doctor. She was
getting older; she knew she had to put a lid on the pot
of rage that boiled over too often in her chest.

Now, more than ever, "Do what you want. I don't
care," was her mantra, especially after complaining
about something the Doctor was going to do. She
devoted much more time to her pet charities and her
elaborate luncheons and gala affairs. To give the devil
her due, she was at least raising funds for important
causes.

All this was why I had a mixture of emotions the
day she died. I was certainly not happy about it, despite
the harsh manner in which she had treated me and the
mean things she had done to me when I was much
younger. I had become more and more like the Doctor
than I imagined I ever would. Like him, I found I was

able to step back from conflicts, from aggressive or unpleasant people, and question why whatever was happening was happening. I seemed to have a natural instinct for analysis, for explaining. Often this was frustrating to my friends, who thought I should be angrier or want revenge. My tolerance irked them, and there I was analyzing why they felt that way as well.

I had begun to do the same with my AM. In short, I had begun not to sympathize with her, but to understand her. Her failure to get what she wanted from her marriage to the Doctor turned her into the bitter person she was capable of being. The tendencies, the selfishness, was always there, waiting to sprout and take control, but the world she had chosen to be in and the life she led certainly fertilized it.

She would hate me for it, but I had grown to see her as a tragic and pathetic figure. What I knew beyond anything was that I never wanted to be like her, and I think, despite all her efforts to make me envy her, to look up to her, to think of her as successful and beautiful, she knew in her heart that she had failed at that. If there was one more thing she could not tolerate around her, it was certainly pity, and especially pity from someone like me.

I was at a rehearsal for the senior play the night she was killed. The custodian who was on duty at the school came into the theater and told my drama teacher to send me home immediately.

"Your father needs you home right away," was all he said.

My heart pounded with every quick step I took to

leave the building, get into my car, and drive back to the house. When I pulled into the driveway, I saw a half dozen vehicles, some of which I recognized as cars belonging to associates of my father and one belonging to Temple Gidleigh, my AM's best and, to my mind, only friend. She and my AM usually served on the same charity committees.

When I entered the house, I heard the low murmur of conversation from the sitting room. I hurried down the corridor to it, and when everyone saw me standing there, he or she stopped talking. The Doctor, who was seated on the settee, put down the cup of tea he was drinking and rose quickly.

"What's wrong?" I asked. "Why are all these people here?"

He indicated we should continue down the corridor to his office, which we did. When we were inside, he closed the door.

"Some very bad news," he said. "Alberta lost control of her car this evening returning from that fund-raiser for MS. She went off the road at Crowley's Junction and down an embankment, where she struck a tree. She wasn't wearing her seat belt and that damn air bag did not activate. It's preliminary, but it looks pretty much as if she struck the windshield and died instantly."

I felt my stomach fold up inside me, my heart tightening like a fist, making it very hard to breathe.

"She's gone," he added, to be sure I understood the full meaning of what he was telling me.

"Gone?" I repeated, like someone trying to memorize what she had been told.

"I'm sorry," he said. For a moment it was as if he were a total stranger giving me the bad news. "These will be difficult days ahead. The funeral will be in three days. My secretary is contacting everyone whom we should contact."

"What should I do?" I asked him.

"There is nothing for you to do, Willow. Death is the most traumatic event in life because of its finality. I spend a good deal of my professional time trying to convince depressed and sick people that it is not the best alternative." He smiled. "I often use Shakespeare and quote from *Hamlet*. 'That undiscovered country from whose bourne no traveler has returned.' I try to get them to see they won't necessarily be better off.

"You have not been brought up in a religious home," he continued, "but I have to believe that she is in a better place. I won't ever tell any of my patients such a thing," he said, smiling again.

Then he put his arm around my shoulders, squeezed me to him, kissed my forehead, and left to return to his and my AM's friends, whom, he said, needed him to comfort them almost as much as he needed them to comfort him.

Without my Amou, I was left to find comfort in myself, for no matter what my true feelings were about Alberta, she and the Doctor were all the family I had, and Death had come into this house.

It made me think of Scott Lawrence and his belief that some people weren't supposed to have mothers and fathers. Death had done its duty.

For all I knew, it still lingered here somewhere,

smiling through its icy teeth, enjoying what it had accomplished.

What it had accomplished was to remind us all It was always there.

It was there waiting for us as well.

# 5

# Setting Sail

What was most remarkable to me after Alberta's death was how little our lives changed. If anything, the Doctor became even more involved in his clinic and with his patients. I was his little amateur psychiatrist by now, and my analysis told me that, despite what he might say to others and how he might seem to be, he was suffering some guilt.

How Alberta's death could have been caused in even the slightest way by him was a mystery that would take some time to unravel. I saw it in the darkness in his eyes whenever he was home, in the hours and hours he spent alone in his office gazing out the window, in the longer walks he took by himself on our grounds, and in the exhaustion he showed in his face whenever he returned from the clinic.

I wrote to Amou about him and spoke to her on the phone from time to time. All she would say was "take care of him," which was of course what she had told me in the airport the day she had left. I knew in my heart that she held some trust with him, that there were still secrets to unfold and surprises awaiting me in the days and years to come.

About three months after my AM's accident and death, Aunt Agnes's husband Uncle Darwood died. I didn't know him very well. They had visited us so rarely and we never visited them. The Doctor and I went to the funeral. Afterward, he revealed that Uncle Darwood had been a bad closet alcoholic. He let slip that he thought Aunt Agnes was the reason, and then we talked about her and him for a while. It was a warm and interesting conversation for me because he did not often talk about his youth and his own parents. He revealed that my AM thought his family was snobby because she came from an old Southern family that had lost most of its wealth. She always accused Aunt Agnes of speaking down to her.

The intensity of the undercurrent of tension and friction that ran under the foundation of our home and family always surprised me. Everyone believed I came from the most stable family possible because my father was a world-renowned psychiatrist who could cure psychological and emotional problems. Some of those problems were so deeply embedded in the roots of our world, however, it was naive to think anyone, even the Doctor, could stop the erosion of happiness and contentment. It was a lesson I was never to forget.

It seemed that there was so little lately to bring any pleasure and satisfaction into our house, but the Doctor was happy that I had been accepted to the University of North Carolina. I had already decided that I wanted to follow in his footsteps to some extent and major in psychology, and he was not only familiar with their programs, but knew some of the teachers I would have.

One of the few prolonged periods of time that he and I were together was when he accompanied me to college. All during the trip he talked about how someone should work at orienting himself or herself to a new environment. His favorite expression was always "Focus, focus."

I thought he was the one doing most of the focusing on that trip, and I was quite pleasantly surprised at how much emotion he finally showed when we parted and he was leaving me at college. He saw me unpack some of my things and noted that I had brought my doll along, the doll he had given me a long time ago, the one a patient had made in his clinic.

"You brought this," he said, holding it and turning it in his hands as if he wanted to inspect every single stitch.

"Yes."

He smiled at it.

"Whatever happened to the patient who made that?" I asked.

He looked up quickly. "Oh, she improved enough to go home eventually. She's never had to come back," he added.

"Maybe I should send that to her," I suggested.

"Oh, no, no," he said. "She wanted you to have it very much. She made it from a picture of you I had sent her after she left the clinic, actually."

"Yes," I said, nodding. "Besides, she probably doesn't want to be reminded she had to be in a clinic once."

"No," he said. "I don't imagine she does."

He put the doll down gently and then turned to me. "I guess it's time to go," he said.

"Okay," I said. I hugged him.

His eyes welled up with tears and all he could say was "Well, well, well."

I kissed him and held tightly to him and assured him I would be fine.

"Of course you will," he said.

When he left, I watched him go off in a taxicab to the airport. I stood there for a moment, wondering why it was that we had lived in a house where emotions had to be kept under tight reins. What was it he feared so? I couldn't imagine the Doctor afraid of anything that much. I wondered to myself if I wasn't going into psychology hoping that I would learn enough to finally understand him.

And then I thought, perhaps I want to go into psychology not so much to learn about him as to learn about myself. So often and in so many ways, Alberta had drummed into my head that I showed signs of inheriting madness. It got so I questioned every action I took, every decision I made, every thought I had. Was it abnormal? Was it the symptom of something developing? Was my childhood pretending really just that—pretending—or was it the first sign of schizophrenia? And those fears I had, seeing something ominous in the shapes of shadows, in the silhouette of a tree at night, outlined against the inky sky, was all that the beginning of serious paranoia?

Were the voices I heard the voices everyone heard? Were my periods of depression and sadness unusual? What really awaited me as I turned the corner and entered adulthood: a life of fulfillment, marriage, a career, motherhood, or the dark corridors of rooms in my father's clinic?

I never told my father, but deep inside, I believed that if I could see the symptoms before anyone else, I could cure them, or maybe hide them well enough to keep even someone like him from knowing. Looking at my doll now, turning it in my hands as my father had done, I felt like a criminal who had gone into forensic science just so she could cover up any clues she might leave behind. Was the likeness to me just a wonderful accident of fate, or did this doll with its dark eyes, its patchwork of a dress speak to my own patchwork of emotions and my own dark fears?

Perhaps I didn't have the most altruistic reasons to go into psychology, but I couldn't see myself doing anything else. If I had inherited anything, I thought, it was the desire to prove Alberta wrong, or at least keep anyone from knowing she had been right.

I had a good first year at college. I met someone, a young man named Allan Simpson, and we began to see each other regularly. We had met at a college mixer when I was a freshman. Barely eighteen at the time, I was hardly a worldly woman and, unlike most of my girlfriends, could easily count on one hand how many boys I had even cared to consider as boyfriends. I used to worry I was incapable of a serious relationship, but the truth was most of the boys I had known always seemed immature to me. Maybe I was too demanding, expecting somehow to find a younger version of the Doctor: serious but not solemn, confident, but not arrogant.

Allan seemed that way to me the first time I had met him. Besides his being a very good-looking man with a strong, masculine mouth, a perfect nose in size and shape, and strikingly dark blue eyes, Allan had a sureness about him, a steady focus that caused him to stand head and shoulders above the young college men around me, who were still very obvious and insecure. Their laughter gushed like broken water pipes. Their courage came from beer and whiskey and shattered in the morning with the light of reality. Like vampires, they avoided mirrors. *If they are so disappointing to themselves,* I thought, *what would they be to me?*

Allan was the first really deep romance of my life. I told the Doctor about him when I returned for a spring break. Our phone conversations were growing longer, and I noticed we were spending more and more time together whenever I did return home.

All he would say about it was, "Be careful with your trust. When you lose it, it's not easy to get it back."

One day during my spring break, he and I sat outside on the patio after dinner and talked for hours. I felt closer to him than ever because he talked about himself as well.

"I'm so glad you're enjoying college, Willow," he began that warm spring evening. The stars burned like the tips of candle flames, growing stronger with every passing minute.

"I am. I love all my classes and enjoy my teachers. In fact, some of my new friends think I'm too serious about my work."

He laughed. "I remember that I had to work so hard to enable myself to attend the university that I would feel some sort of ridiculous guilt if I relished my studies and wallowed with pleasure in my assignments and challenges."

"That's how I feel."

"It wasn't supposed to be fun," he continued, gazing out at the fields and the lake and forest beyond as if he could look past the present, back in time to happier days. His smile said all that.

"It was supposed to be hard work," he continued. "What an incredibly unexpected reaction to it all. Like your new friends, some of my closer friends thought I was bizarre. 'Psychiatry is a good place for you, Claude,' they would say. 'Eventually, you can treat yourself and send yourself the bill.'"

We both laughed at the idea, and then he turned to me, his face as serious as it had ever been.

"If we don't love what we do," he told me, "then we don't love who we are, and the worst fate of all is not liking yourself, Willow, being trapped in a body and behind a face you despise. You hate the sound of your own voice. You even come to hate your own shadow. How can you ever hope to make anyone else happy— wife, children, friends—if you can't make yourself happy?

"It seems like such a simple truth, but it remains buried beneath so many lies and delusions for most people. I know now that won't happen to you," he said assuredly.

I sensed he was going to tell me more, but Miles appeared to tell him he had a phone call from the clinic.

"They say it's an emergency," he added.

The crisis involved a patient who had attempted suicide. The Doctor had to rush back to the clinic. He was very upset about it, and told me afterward that he thought he had been making some significant progress with the patient, who was a young man my age. Although he didn't show it often, my doctor father did take his work very personally.

"If you are serious about going into this field, Willow," he warned, "be prepared for more defeat than victory, more failure than success. There is no more complicated thing than the human mind and try- ing to determine why people do what they do, want what they want, and hate what they hate. Unlike a medical doctor, your patients more often than not are unwilling to let you discover what is the cause of their illness. They are either afraid or unable to do so. Imagine a doctor's patient preventing the doctor from knowing he or she has a fever, and refusing to let the doctor take his or her temperature, and then you will have a little better idea of what awaits you in the world of psychiatry."

"I understand," I said, "and I am not discouraged."

He smiled. "Good," he said. He closed and opened his eyes. "That's very good."

I returned to finish my college semester. Allan and I continued seeing each other. I didn't want to fall in love so fast. The Doctor's words stayed with me. More than ever now, I was very determined to develop a career first. During the summer, Allan went to Europe to study, and I didn't see him again until the start of the new semester. I thought we would drift apart and he would probably find someone else, but to my surprise and delight at the time, that wasn't so.

It was the Doctor's idea that I do some volunteer work at his clinic that summer. I think I learned more about psychology in those ten weeks than I did or would in four years of formal schooling. One thing that happened was my appreciation and respect for him grew. His reputation in the world of psychology had only grown over the years, and he was off as a guest speaker more often than ever.

My working there brought us even closer. We spent more time together after work as well, going to restaurants, taking walks on our grounds, or simply relaxing and watching some televison. I could feel his effort to get to know me more and to slowly lower the barriers that had been kept up between us for so many years. One of the first things that happened was I stopped thinking of him as the Doctor, and, finally, as my father. After all, he was the only father I had known. Whoever had made my real mother pregnant did not know I existed, much less cared, and if there was one thing I had learned from Scott Lawrence and his family, it was that relationships, not blood, mattered the most.

When I prepared to leave for college this time, I did not expect it would be as emotional for either of us. We were planning to have dinner at my father's favorite restaurant. He had made all the arrangements, and I sensed it was going to be a special night for us. Two days before, however, he received a phone call from the coordinator of the American Psychiatry Association, who informed him their schedule for the upcoming national conference had been revised because the feature speaker, set to greet everyone, had suffered a heart attack. They wanted my father, and since he would have a national forum from which he could reveal and discuss some of his innovative techniques at his clinic, he had to accept. With the work he had to complete before leaving, his free time was constricted.

"Don't worry," I told him. "We'll see each other very soon anyway. Remember, you promised to visit me on campus this semester so I could show you off," I said, and he laughed.

He was gone the day before I left for school. Alone in the big house, except for Miles and the maid who came by to clean twice a week, I wandered slowly through the big estate home and thought about my youth here, my Amou, and my AM. I felt guilty calling her that now, but it just seemed to come naturally to me.

So much of this house still seemed off-limits to me or still carried unhappy memories. It was here in the family room that Alberta came upon me one afternoon. I was pretending to be a mother and I was mothering two small dolls. I suppose I was imitating her too well, for she stood behind me quietly, listened, and then pounced.

She told me I was sick in the head to think such terrible things at my age, and she warned me if she ever caught me doing it again, she would put glue in my mouth and make my tongue stick to the roof of it. It was a terrifying image. I tried not to cry until she left because she hated that. It only made her angrier.

Because of that and a few other occasions when she spied upon me, I took to whispering my pretend, even when I was outside and there was no chance of her overhearing any of it.

The Doctor had kept her things in the bedroom for a long time after she died, mostly because he just didn't have the time to get around to doing anything about it, I thought, but I also thought it was because removing her clothing, her cosmetics, her brushes and all would be like closing the lid on her coffin, and it was just something he was avoiding for as long as he could.

Now, her naked vanity desk remained, a cold reminder of what had once been. Of course, I recalled the infamous time she caught me in her makeup and revealed the great secret of my birth and status. I could see myself sitting there as a little girl, enjoying my pretend, and I could see her in the doorway, furious.

The Doctor's office would always remain sacrosanct to me. His personality was there, in its order and neatness. *Alberta never liked coming in here,* I thought. It actually was threatening to her. Maybe that was why I enjoyed being in there so much. In our house, this office was like a sanctuary. Evil, nastiness, anger, and pain were not permitted within its doors. Here there was only calmness, reason, logic, concern.

Amou's room was now occupied by Miles, because it was much nicer than the room he had had when she was living here. Still, just walking down that corridor and looking at the door brought back so many, many memories of her. I was so attached to her. I loved just watching her work, whether it was in the kitchen or doing her needlepoint. Her voice was forever embedded in my mind—those melodies, Portuguese folk songs, children's songs, and her laughter, melodic, full of love and life. It still echoed in this hallway. It would never be gone.

I wandered to the rear door and stepped out on the patio. The sun was setting. This would be the last twilight here for me for a while. Despite the difficult childhood I had experienced growing up here, it was still home. I knew no other, and at least I had a home, a place to call my own, or as Robert Frost once wrote, "A place where when you go there, they have to take you in."

Even if it was no more than that, it was something.

I had this great faith that, in the days and weeks, months and years to come, the Doctor—my father—and I would grow into a true father and daughter, and this house, these grounds would warm up considerably for me. There would be a time when we would truly just have each other, and that would be enough for both of us for a while.

I would get married and have a family of my own. I was very determined about that, too, as determined as I was to have a career. It was as if I thought I could get revenge for how I had been treated. *My child will drown in my love,* I thought. There would never be a doubt as to whom his or her mother was. It made me laugh to think of myself that way, but there was something inside me that called for and demanded that.

Can we be forgiven for giving too much love?

*We certainly can't be for giving too little,* I thought angrily.

Then I imagined the Doctor beside me shaking his head.

"Anger isn't appropriate for a therapist, Willow," he would tell me. "Step back, analyze. You don't have to forgive, but you do have to understand."

I sighed and nodded.

*All right,* I thought. *I'll try to do that . . . always.*

*But I might not be as strong as you.*

The Doctor.

My father.

My friend.

*Will you forgive me for that at least?*

My thoughts were caught up in the wind that stirred

with the descending sunlight. Shadows were emerging from the woods, marching toward the house. It was almost their time. Night waited anxiously to put the birds asleep and put our thoughts in bed with us.

We all have little boxes in which we lock them all, our thoughts and memories, and keep them shut until someone like the Doctor, or maybe me someday, gives us the courage and the faith to open them again and let them go free.

After all, who wants to be chained by his or her own memories?

I turned back to the house.

*I will not let that happen to me,* I thought.

*I will open my heart and release my pain. I will bury it with the past in a grave as deep and as dark as Alberta's grave.*

*Only then will the Doctor and I find true peace.*

I did not know why this should be so.

But soon.

Soon I would.

And then it would all begin.

# THE SHOOTING STARS SERIES

# VIRGINIA ANDREWS

## SHOOTING STARS

Cinnamon, Ice, Rose and Honey; four talented
girls with troubled pasts who will one day come
together . . .

Available in hardback April 2005

## FALLING STARS

The spellbinding sequel to *Shooting Stars*. All the
world's a stage – but what if the play doesn't go as
planned?

Available in hardback August 2005

SIMON &
SCHUSTER

# Shooting Stars

### Four talented girls share a dream of stardom . . .

**Cinnamon**'s daydreams are her only escape from her Mother's breakdowns and her grandmother's over-bearing control. But Cinnamon is discovering something special about herself: a talent for the theatre which might finally give her a chance to escape.

**Ice** hides from the world behind a shield of silence. And that's what her mother hates about her. All she wants is a normal daughter who wears make-up and wears sexy clothes. But Ice gets her chance to shine when she reveals her beautiful shining voice.

Beautiful and talented **Rose** was the apple of her father's eye. But when he is tragically taken from her, his carefully hidden secrets destroy the only life she's ever known.

**Honey** grew up on a farm under her strictly religious Grandfather's disapproving eye. To him, *everything* is a sin – from Honey's talent for the violin to her innocent interest in boys and dating. But then a shocking family secret comes to light and Honey discovers the startling cause of her grandfather's bitter fury.

**ISBN 0 7432 5223 3**
**PRICE £17.99**

SIMON &
SCHUSTER

# Falling Stars

Four talented girls from vastly different pasts share a
dream of stardom: Cinnamon, the edgy actress; Ice, the
phenomenal vocalist; Rose, the beautiful dancer; and
Honey, the first-rate violinist. The four meet at the
prestigious Senetsky School of the Performing Arts –
housed in an ornate New York mansion – and become
instant friends as they take off on a dazzling whirlwind of
intense classes, theatre outings and celebrity-studded
parties.

But they soon realise this is no ordinary school. Madame
Senetsky pushes the girls' studies beyond reason. She
controls their social lives. And they get the strange
feeling someone is watching them. But who? And why?
Cinnamon, Ice, Rose and Honey set out to untangle a
shadowy web of Senetsky family secrets. As they explore
dark corners and hidden rooms, every creak and moan of
the old mansion tells a story too frightening to repeat. A
devastating story that could destroy their dreams.

ISBN 0 7432 2131 1

PRICE £17.99

POCKET
BOOKS

This book and other **Virginia Andrews** titles are available from your book shop or can be ordered direct from the publisher.

Please send cheque or postal order for the value
of the book, **free postage and packing within
the UK**, to: SIMON & SCHUSTER CASH SALES
PO Box 29, Douglas, Isle of Man, IM99 1BQ
Tel: 01624 677237, Fax 01624 670923
bookshop@enterprise.net
www.bookpost.co.uk

Please allow 14 days for delivery. Prices and availability subject
to change without notice.